BOTCHAN

Sōseki Natsume (1867–1916) is widely considered the foremost novelist of the Meiji period (1868–1914). After graduating from Tokyo Imperial University in 1893, Sōseki taught high school before spending two years in England on a Japanese government scholarship. He returned to lecture in English literature at the university. Numerous nervous disorders forced him to give up teaching in 1908 and he became a full-time writer for the *Asahi* newspaper. In addition to fourteen novels, Sōseki wrote haiku, poems in the Chinese style, academic papers on literary theory, essays, autobiographical sketches, and fairy tales.

Sōseki Natsume

BOTCHAN

Translated by Umeji Sasaki
With a new Introduction by Dennis Washburn

TUTTLE Publishing
Tokyo | Rutland, Vermont | Singapore

ABOUT TUTTLE
"Books to Span the East and West"

Our core mission at Tuttle Publishing is to create books which bring people together one page at a time. Tuttle was founded in 1832 in the small New England town of Rutland, Vermont (USA). Our fundamental values remain as strong today as they were then—to publish best-in-class books informing the English-speaking world about the countries and peoples of Asia. The world has become a smaller place today and Asia's economic, cultural and political influence has expanded, yet the need for meaningful dialogue and information about this diverse region has never been greater. Since 1948, Tuttle has been a leader in publishing books on the cultures, arts, cuisines, languages and literatures of Asia. Our authors and photographers have won numerous awards and Tuttle has published thousands of books on subjects ranging from martial arts to paper crafts. We welcome you to explore the wealth of information available on Asia at **www.tuttlepublishing.com**.

Published by Tuttle Publishing, an imprint of Periplus Editions (HK) Ltd.

www.tuttlepublishing.com

First Tuttle edition, 1968

Library of Congress Cataloging-in-Publication Data in process

ISBN 978-4-8053-1263-6

22 21 20 19   7 6 5 4 3   1908MP
Printed in Singapore

TUTTLE PUBLISHING® is a registered trademark of Tuttle Publishing, a division of Periplus Editions (HK) Ltd.

Distributed by

North America, Latin America & Europe
Tuttle Publishing
364 Innovation Drive
North Clarendon,
VT 05759-9436, USA
Tel: 1 (802) 773 8930
Fax: 1 (802) 773 6993
info@tuttlepublishing.com
www.tuttlepublishing.com

Japan
Tuttle Publishing
Yaekari Building 3rd Floor
5-4-12 Osaki Shinagawa-ku
Tokyo 1410032, Japan
Tel: (81) 3 5437 0171
Fax: (81) 3 5437 0755
sales@tuttle.co.jp
www.tuttle.co.jp

Asia Pacific
Berkeley Books Pte Ltd
3 Kallang Sector #04-01
Singapore 349278
Tel: (65) 6741-2178
Fax: (65) 6741-2179
inquiries@periplus.com.sg
www.periplus.com

Introduction

*B*otchan was a major commercial success when it was published in 1906, and it remains to this day one of the most widely read novels in Japan. The book owes its lasting popularity to several factors: the accessible style, the nostalgic (though gently critical) attitude toward Japan's traditions and agrarian past, the comforting familiarity of its stock characters, and, above all, the humorous depiction of situations with which readers today can still identity. The canonical status of the novel is further sustained institutionally, for it is regularly assigned reading for schoolchildren across the country.

Despite its enormous popularity, however, critical assessments of *Botchan* tend to relegate it to minor status within the oeuvre of the author, Natsume Kinnosuke—best known by his pen name, Sōseki. While it is possible to see in such judgments an unconscious bias against broadly comic works, dismissing them on that score would be an over-correction. *Botchan* is skillfully executed in purely stylistic terms, but there can be no doubt that Sōseki's later novels achieve much greater depth in theme and character development. If there is an analogue to the critical reception of *Botchan*, perhaps Mark Twain's *Tom Sawyer* is an apt comparison. No one questions that *Tom Sawyer* is a classic of American letters, but Twain's idyllic portrait of the life of a young boy on the Mississippi pales in comparison to the far more serious and morally engaged (though still humorous) themes he explored in *Huckleberry Finn*. This is not to say that works like *Tom Sawyer* or *Botchan* cannot be read for what they are and on their own terms (though I believe that statement implies an unfair devaluation), but the reputations of these books are undeniably affected by the reception of their authors' subsequent novels. Thus, for contemporary readers to be able to appreciate the literary qualities that made a work like *Botchan*, so popular in Japan, we must consider its place in the author's career and the ways in which its composition actually made the greater novels possible.

During his lifetime, Sōseki was widely honored in East Asia as an enormously influential intellectual and literary figure. However, despite the publication in 1922 of Umeji Sasaki's translation of *Botchan*, he remained largely unknown to the rest of the world until the boom in translations of Japanese literature that took place in the two decades following the Second World War. As more of his writings became widely accessible, the late novels in particular came to be recognized as a major achievement of world literature. The period of time that elapsed between the appearance of Sasaki's translation of *Botchan* and the translations of other works is noteworthy, because that publication history has had a profound effect on the wider perception of the nature of Sōseki's literary art.

As noted just above, Sōseki's current reputation as a serious writer of the first rank is largely based on critical assessments of his last novels— *Kokoro*, *Michikusa* (Grass on the Wayside), and the unfinished *Meian* (The Light and the Dark). This reputation is undoubtedly well deserved, but the sweeping praise of these somber, tragic stories can sometimes obscure other aspects of his career: namely, that Sōseki had not only extraordinary range and commercial viability, but also considerable experimental daring. In this regard, *Botchan*, for all its apparently frivolous qualities, marks a significant milestone in the development of Sōseki's distinctive stylistics and the unique voice and perspective that made him such a trenchant observer of the manners and mores of Japanese society.

Sōseki's temperament as a writer sprang in part from his own experiments in narrative form, but it was also shaped by his personal circumstances. Born in Tokyo in 1867, right on the cusp of the great historical transformations of the Meiji era, he was given up for adoption at the age of two, only to be returned to his birth parents when he was nine. In his later years, Sōseki remarked on the formative nature of this traumatic experience, which became the subject of his last complete novel, *Michikusa*. The unusual circumstances of his upbringing not only shaped his introspective personality, but made him keenly sensitive to the dislocations that afflicted so many of his generation.

His early education stressed the Chinese classics, and he eventually became an accomplished writer of *kanshi*, poetry in Chinese. In 1884 he entered Yoshimon College to study architecture, but transferred to the department of literature at Tokyo Imperial University, graduating in 1892. He finished his graduate studies in English Literature in 1895, and married the following year. After several years spent teaching in the provinces, the Ministry of Education sent him to London in 1900, where he studied for almost three memorably unhappy years. Upon his return to Japan in 1903, he took up the prestigious post of lecturer in English at Tokyo Imperial University. Following the success of his first novels, he surprised his colleagues by resigning this position in 1907 to become a full-time author and the literary editor for the *Asahi* newspaper. His writing career was interrupted in 1910 when he physically collapsed as a result of stomach ulcers. Although he recovered enough to write what many consider his most important novels, chronic bouts of ulcers eventually claimed his life in 1916 at the age of forty-nine.

Sōseki's productivity in the face of chronic depression and health problems—conditions that were often the wellspring of his comic fiction—seems almost amazing, especially when we consider that his career as a novelist spanned a single productive decade, beginning in 1905 with the serialization of *Wagahai wa neko de aru* (I am a Cat). This first novel, which consists mainly of humorous vignettes narrated by a cat, presents a satirical view of modernizing bourgeois society. The cat belongs to Mr. Kushami (Mr. Sneeze), a lazy, dyspeptic academic who is in certain respects a self-mocking portrait of the author himself. The early installments were extremely popular, not only because of the freshness of their depiction of the foibles of Meiji society, but also because the anecdotal structure of the novel, which was closer to the literary practices of the Edo period (1600-1868) than to Western realistic novels, possessed a comfortable familiarity that appealed to a wide readership. Nonetheless, for all of its ostensibly old-fashioned qualities, *Wagahai wa neko de aru* reflects the general Meiji project of modernizing literary practices by abandoning ornate language in favor of a standardized style based on the speech patterns of the Tokyo dialect.

Sōseki continued experimenting with this vernacular style in *Botchan*, which depicts in broad narrative brushstrokes the travails of a sincere young man who, though not very bright himself, ends up teaching high school in the provinces. Sōseki drew on his own experience as a teacher—though in fairness, it must be noted that his students and the locals treated him quite well (unlike the treatment accorded his protagonist). Still, for all the farcical elements that distinguish the novel, there are serious undercurrents. The protagonist, an orphan dispossessed of his family's former status as samurai, is a prototype of the rootless young man who comes to figure prominently in Sōseki's later fiction. More important, the writing of *Botchan* marked the beginning of a highly experimental and productive period during which the author developed the stylistics that would become the hallmark of his mature novels.

For readers today, Sōseki's experimental turn is perhaps more clearly recognizable in the novels that immediately followed the publication of *Botchan*. *Kusamakura* (literally, Pillow of Grass, 1906) is formally much different from his first two novels. Sōseki referred to it as a novel in the manner of a haiku, and certain passages resemble the *haibun*, or poetic journals, of the great Edo poets Bashō and Buson. The narrator is a Tokyo painter who comes to a village in the mountains to work and is attracted to a mysterious young woman, Onami, whose apparent lack of passion is the inspiration for his lyrical evocations of place and his musings on the nature of art. In *Nowaki* (1907: An Autumn Tempest), Sōseki begins moving toward the psychological realism that would eventually distinguish his mature style. The story depicts the relationships between Takayanagi, a poor young man who is dying of tuberculosis, Shirai, a poor teacher, and a wealthy man named Nakano. The melodramatic quality of the story is grounded in class tensions and hatred of the rich, but Sōseki achieves an edgy depth in his characterization of Takayanagi, who realizes that Shirai's hatred is born of political principle, while his own is born of envy. Takayanagi's growing self-awareness forces him to acknowledge his spiritual emptiness and leads him to sacrifice his ambitions and his health for the sake of Shirai.

Interestingly, the next novel, *Gubijinsō* (1907: Red Poppy), is a throwback to the didactic novels of late Edo in its plotting, characterization, and heavily Sinicized language. For all his skepticism about traditional culture, which he viewed as backward and potentially dangerous, Sōseki was also ambivalent about completely abandoning the practices of pre-Meiji literature in favor of Western modes of representation; and that ambivalence is apparent in his peculiar misogynistic obsession with the character Fujio, who is a Neo-Confucian version of a *femme fatale*. This obsession is apparent in his journals where he insists that he must kill off this character. As it turned out, *Gubijinsō* was a reluctant purging of traditional literary values and practices in pursuit of a narrative mode that made it possible for him to write.

Kōfu (1908: The Miner) was yet another radical stylistic departure that left many critics at the time befuddled. The story of a troubled young man who runs away from home and finds work in a mine is also an exploration of the art of the novel through parodic treatments of narrative conventions, including the conventions of the poetic journal. The descent into the hellish world of the mine is ultimately redemptive for the protagonist, but this tale is so overtly framed by the narrative's concerns with the nature of literary art that it struck some contemporary readers as avant-garde.

Finally, with *Sanshirō* (1908) Sōseki settles into a distinctive narrative mode that enables him to fully explore the theme of the loneliness of the individual in modern Japan. Because his style in this Bildungsroman is a tightly controlled psychological realism, its novelty, like that of *Botchan*, may be especially easy to overlook. The narrative techniques that Sōseki developed between 1906 and 1908 are at once original and unsettling, part commentary on and part product of the profound cultural tensions of the literary milieu in which he worked.

From the vantage of this slightly wider view of Sōseki's career, the novels of his final years are for the most part elaborations on, rather than radical shifts away from, the styles he played with and the themes he explored in his formative period. As mentioned earlier, the most notable feature of his final novels is their increasingly dark and pessimistic tone. The problem of moral confusion and the pessimism that became increasingly prominent elements in his writing might have been the result of his failing health, but that explanation of the source of his inspiration is not by itself adequate. Rather, Sōseki's propensity for narrative experimentation is more likely the source of his attempts to fully explore the darker implications of modernity. In the open-ended process of searching for a distinctive voice, Sōseki created a compelling vision of the struggles the individual faced as a result of the cultural discontinuity of Meiji Japan.

It is this serious, darker author that the Treasury of Japan chose to honor in 1984 when it decided to grace the thousand-Yen note with an idealized portrait of Sōseki. That decision certainly provides a fine example of the unintended irony only a bureaucracy can produce, but it is also an example of how critical praise based on a single aspect of an author's work can obscure other aspects of a rich, complicated career. The Japanese government chose for the symbol of its powerful economy an artist who critiqued the shallow ambitions of materialist culture, and it made an icon of a man who relentlessly resisted, with both gentle humor and caustic satire, modern inclinations to hero-worship.

In *Botchan* it is Sōseki the artist, not the culture-hero, whose sensibility is on full display. There is nothing stuffy about acknowledging that comic fiction can be serious literature. *Botchan* is an amusement, and it is an admirable work of art that is of a

piece with the rest of Sōseki's canon. In recognizing that re-
markable achievement, one final observation on this particular
edition is in order. Translators are usually overlooked when dis-
cussing the merits of a work, but the efforts of Umeji Sasaki
deserve mention. His language is careful and precise, even
slightly prim and formal, and the tension between that style and
the contents of the narrative is extremely effective in conveying
the arch, comic tone of the original. There are now several
translations of *Botchan*—including an exceptionally fine version by Joel Cohn—and the recent spate of interest in making
this novel available in English speaks to its enduring appeal. For
those who cannot read the novel in Japanese, the presence of
multiple translations is extraordinarily helpful, but there is
much to recommend Sasaki's rendering. Though it is the earliest version in English, it retains a charm and freshness that
brings the text to life.

Dennis C. Washburn
Jane and Raphael Bernstein Professor in Asian Studies
Dartmouth College

Publisher's Foreword

In his foreword written in 1922, translator Umeji Sasaki commented on the changes even then overtaking Japan. Now, years later, the Old Japan has given way to the New. Recent decades have witnessed vast changes in customs and attitudes.

Although it was written in 1904, *Botchan* is an enduring novel because the young man who dominates the story typifies the fascinating combination of old idealism with modern independence. Today we would call Botchan a "loner." In his time he would have been described as an individualist. Whatever the designation, his qualities as a person have won him a lasting place in twentieth century literature. One cannot help admire his tenacity, his perversity and, above all, his optimism.

In reissuing this modern classic in an English edition, we are pleased to provide to a new generation of readers the opportunity to read this timeless work by Sōseki Natsume.

Foreword

"A book may be amusing with numerous errors, or it may be very dull without a single absurdity." Of all the novels written by Sōseki, *Botchan* is the most popular among young people. The hero in this story unites in himself contradictory traits of character: he is rash, driving, hasty; he is like a locomotive puffing and pulling; yet he is honest, simple and frank. He never says or does what he does not mean. He never flatters, he is "Yes" or "No." There is no halfway in him. Young folks cannot read the book without loving him.

Old Japan with her polite, yet often deceptive, ways is passing to return no more, and New Japan with her honest, simple, frank democratic ways must come to speak and act in world terms. Botchan, the hero of the book, is in many respects a young man embodying the new ideals of New Japan. Sōseki was prophetic in delineating such a character in the book. As for Principal Badger, Red-shirt, Noda, the Clown, Madonna, Green Squash, Porcupine, *et al.*, let them speak for themselves. Personal fidelity, a relic of Old Japan, is significantly held up by the author in the old woman Kiyo, the hero's nurse. Her letter four feet long addressed to her young master is one of the finest letters I have ever read.

日当りや
　熟柿の如き
　　思あり　　　　　　漱石

Hiatari-ya
　Jukushi no gotoki
　　Omoi ari.

I was basking in the sun;
I felt like a ripe persimmon.　　　Sōseki.

Sōseki was a true poet. He was happy and contented as he could enjoy the sunshine. He could do without fame or gold, but the sun's rays were his manna. Bathing in the sun, he felt as if he were a ripe persimmon. Wonderful imagination! He would have asked the same favor of an Alexander as Diogenes, the great Greek philosopher, "Sire, won't you please get away a little from the sun? I have nothing more to ask of you." Lolling luxuriously in the sun, giving full liberty to his limbs, he often blinked lazily up at the sun. He was ready to burst out like a ripe persimmon. Even the greedy crow would not venture near, lest it should burst like a mine.

Being a poet, he is always suggestive, and this suggestiveness so often flashes out like lightning in *Botchan;* and the translator has done his best in retaining it in the translation.

The rattan sofa on the veranda of his study is shown to the visitor at the home of Japan's literary star, in Minamicho, Waseda. I was charmed to see that sofa on which the novelist used to take a sun bath. The little ebony desk with an inkstand, a pen, and paper is patiently waiting for its owner to come and sit there as if it knew not of his departure from the earth.

Sincere thanks are due to Mrs. Natsume, who so generously allowed me to translate *Botchan;* and I feel very grateful to Prof. E. W. Clement of the First National College who has so kindly looked over my translation.

UMEJI SASAKI.
January 4, 1922.

Chapter 1

A great loser have I been ever since a child, having a rash, daring spirit, a spirit I inherited from my ancestors. When a primary-school boy, I jumped down from the second story of the schoolhouse, and had to lie abed about a week. Some may be curious enough as to ask me why I did such a rash thing. I had no special reason. I had one day been looking down from the window of the second story of the new school, when one of my classmates looked up and said in a taunt.

"You are a great boaster. But you cannot jump down from that height. You poor little creeping thing!" My father, seeing me come home on the back of the janitor, said in an angry tone that no strong boy could be hurt by jumping down from such a low height as from upstairs, and I assured him that he would be proud to see me come out all right next time.

A foreign-made penknife had been given me by one of my relations, and I was showing it proudly to my comrades, the bright blades reflecting the sunlight, when one of the boys said that bright as it shone it was a dull knife after all. I told him that it was sharp and I could cut anything with it. "Well," said he, "try it on your finger!" "Look here," said I, and I tried it on the thumb of my right hand. It bled much, but fortunately the knife being small and the bone solid, the finger has retained its original position to this day although I shall carry the scar to my grave.

Twenty steps east in the yard of my house, there was a small garden sloping up southward, where stood a chestnut tree. This was the tree prized by me even more than life itself. At its fruiting time, the tree found me an early riser who would come out into the back yard in a nightgown, and gather the brown nuts on the ground; these I would take to school to eat.

Kantarō, a thirteen-year-old boy, was the son of Yamashiroya, a pawnbroker, whose yard was next to ours on the west. He was a feeble boy, yet he would come and steal the fruit, climbing over the bamboo fence, which formed the boundary between the two premises. One afternoon toward dusk, hiding myself behind the folding wicket, I caught the thief at last. Losing the way back, Kantarō, came plunging toward me with the strength and courage of a desperate mouse fleeing a cat. He was two years older and stronger than I, though a weak-hearted, spiritless boy. Placing his flat crowned head against my chest, he pushed me with all his might, but his head slipped and came into the sleeve of my lined garment. Finding it very inconvenient in using my arm, I tried very hard to shake it off, the head moving right and left like a pendulum each time. Out of agony, he at last bit me on the arm in the sleeve. Great pain gave me great strength, and I hurled him down against the fence by coiling my leg around his. Fully six feet below our garden, were the premises of Yamashiroya. Kantarō, breaking half of the fence, fell head over heels down to his own domain, a suppressed scream escaping from his half-choked throat. The sleeve of my garment went with him when he fell over, and I found my arm free. That evening my mother went to the pawnbroker's to apologize, and begged back the lost sleeve.

Besides these, I did many other naughty things. Once I took Kanekō, a carpenter's apprentice boy, and Kaku, a fish-monger's boy, to the carrot patch belonging to a certain Mosaku. Rice straw being scattered over the spots where the carrot sprouts had not come out evenly, we found the place a ready-made ring, and spent half of the day in wrestling, thus ruining the whole field. Again, I had the disgrace of being exposed to shame by clogging the well spout in the rice field owned by a certain person named Furukawa. A long bamboo tube, the joints of which were well bored, had been buried perpendicularly deep into the ground; water came out from the spout and flowed into the rice field. Not knowing at the time it was such a contrivance of great moment, I filled it up with pebbles and sticks of all sizes and shapes by putting one after another into the spout. Satisfied to see no water ooze out, I returned home and was having supper, when Furukawa in great rage came roaring into the house; a certain sum of money was paid as a fine to pacify the angry man.

I was not a bit loved by father; mother's favorite was my elder brother. This brother had a complexion unpleasantly white, verging almost on paleness; he was very fond of theatrical performances, and would play the part of a female. Every time father saw me, he would say, "This fellow is the black sheep of the family." Mother would be very anxious about my future, saying I would never be good, being so very unruly. Their prophecy was right to a certain extent. I am neither great nor good, as you see. It was quite right that both my parents were very much worried about my future career. The only consolation is that I have not yet been put into prison for hard labor.

Two or three days before mother died of an illness, I was turning somersaults in the kitchen, and had my ribs hurt by striking them against the corner of the oven, which gave me great pain. Mother, getting very angry, said she did not wish to see me any more, and I was sent to my relation's to stay until I received further notice from home. The notice came to me in an entirely unexpected form. It was the news of mother's death. I had not expected the event would happen so soon. I returned home, wishing I had been a better boy while she was so seriously ill. My elder brother, finding me home again, said that I was an ungrateful son; that mother had died so soon because of me. Too much to bear, I gave him a good slap on the cheek, for which I got a hard scolding afterward.

After mother's death, we three lived together; father, brother, and I. Father would do nothing, and whenever he saw me he would tell me that I was a good-for-nothing fellow. I have, however, been unable to see the reason why I was such a useless boy; I can tell you he was a strange father. Brother was studying English very hard, expecting to be a businessman. His was a character both effeminate and deceitful, and we never were friends. We fell out about once every ten days. One time we played a game of chess. He cowardly set a chessman in ambush and used many insulting words as if he were glad to see me greatly embarrassed. Finding it too hard to bear, I hurled the *hisha* (a chessman of great importance) I held in my hand at his forehead; a few drops of blood came out of the wound it made. He went and told father, who said he would turn me out of the house right away.

Thinking it could not be helped this time, I had been expecting to be disinherited any moment, when the woman-servant named Kiyo who had served in our family for the past ten years came to my rescue, and pleaded in tears so earnestly for me to the angry father that I was spared the disgrace of being turned out of the family. However, I was not afraid of father; I was rather sorry for the sake of Kiyo, the servant. This old woman, I was told, came from a decent family, whose fortune had been ruined at the time of the Restoration, and thus came to serve in our family. I do not know what affinity there was in our previous states of existence, yet she was so fond of me that I thought it very strange. Three days before mother died, I was already a hopeless case to her. Father thought me unruly and beyond his control all the year round; the people of the ward I lived in turned their faces away from me as a branded bad boy; still I was Kiyo's great favorite. Believing I was born to be hated, I did not take it amiss to be ill treated like a chip of wood, and rather thought it strange to be so much loved by Kiyo. When the coast was clear, she would often praise me, saying, "You have a fine character straight as an arrow." I could, however, hardly understand what she meant. Had I had the fine character she said I had, other people should also have treated me a little more kindly. Each time Kiyo said such nice things to me, I would tell her that I hated sweet words. Upon this, the old woman would look into my face admiringly, and was happy to say that very thing more than anything else was ample proof of my having a nice character. It seemed as if she had created me by her own power and were proud of her handiwork. I felt rather suspicious.

After mother's death, I was loved by Kiyo more than ever. It seemed strange even to my young mind that she was so fond of me. I thought I was too worthless to be caressed, and she had better stop it. I felt sorry about her; still I was dear to her. Often she would buy me doughnuts and crackers with her scanty pocket money; on cold nights she would make porridge from the buckwheat flour she had secretly laid in and bring it to my bedside unnoticed. Even a pot of hot macaroni often found its way to my room. Not only these treats, but also stockings, pencils, and notebooks were bought for me by Kiyo. Much later than the time I am describing, she brought me three yen. I had not asked her for it; she came to my room herself and said I might be short of pocket money and the sum was at my service. Of course I told her I did not need it, but as she insisted upon my accepting it, I accepted it from her. To tell the truth, I was very glad to have it. I put the money into my purse, and went to wash my hands, carelessly thrusting the purse into the breastfolds of my clothes and dropped it down the toilet. Not knowing what to do, I came out of the bathroom very much embarrassed, and told Kiyo what had happened to the purse. She said she would get it for me with a bamboo stick. In a little while I heard somebody washing at the well side. I went out and saw Kiyo cleansing the purse by fixing its string to the end of a stick. Then taking the bills out of the purse, we found them all turned yellow, the patterns being a little defaced. Drying them over the brazier, she gave them to me saying that they would do. I told her that they had a bad smell. "Then," said she, "give them to me and I will get them changed." I do not know what tricks she played, but in a short time, she brought back three yen in silver. I do not remember what I did with that money. I told her I would pay it back soon, but the promise has not yet been fulfilled. Now I wish I could return a sum ten times as much as the original, but it remains just a wish.

Kiyo gave me things only when neither father nor brother was at home. Nothing do I dislike more than to get profit myself while others sit empty handed. Brother and I were not friends; still I did not like to get cakes and colored pencils from her without his knowledge. Sometimes I asked her why she was so partial to me, and she would very composedly say that my father bought things for my brother, so she had nothing to do with him. This was not fair on the part of Kiyo. Old fashioned and obstinate as he was, father would never do anything partial nor show anybody favoritism. However, he seemed to be partial

"I told her that they still had a bad smell."

to the prejudiced eye of the old woman whose excessive love to me was anything but fair. And it could not be helped, considering she was an uneducated woman, although she came from a family of some social standing. This was not all. She was firmly convinced that I would get on finely in the world and be a great man in future. This idea came of course from her injudicious liking for me. On the other hand, she said that my brother had a very white complexion, yet a poor future, however hard he might work. She believed there lay a great future before one whom she liked, while ruin awaited those whom she hated.

I had never thought what I would be, yet as Kiyo said I would be great, I thought I should be somebody in the world. Exceedingly foolish it seems to me now. Once I asked her what I should be, but she had no special idea on that point; she simply said that I would certainly live in a stately mansion with a beautiful porch and drive out in a fine carriage.

Kiyo had been expecting to live with me when I could have a home of my own. She asked me again and again if I would let her stay with me, and I told her not to worry about that, for she would surely have a home in my new establishment, which I was sure I could set up. Imagination is a happy enchantress: she will put up a fine castle in the air. Kiyo had a brilliant one; she was so very fanciful as to ask me in what part of the city I would like to make a new home. Was it Kōjimachi, or Azabu? She told me to have a swing in the yard, and that only one room of foreign style was enough. She was pleased to arrange things according to her own taste. At that time, I had no desire of having a home, and neither a foreign nor a Japanese house was an attraction to me; each time I told it to her, she would commend me, saying that I was quite unselfish and my mind was just as pure as a crystal. My Kiyo was as full of praises as a nurse is full of pins.

I lived thus for some five or six years after mother died. I got scoldings from father; I often had quarrels with brother, and got cakes from Kiyo with her usual praise. Having no special ambition I thought this mode of life suited me just as well. I believed that other boys had the same experiences as I. But as Kiyo told me so often I was an unfortunate boy, I thought I must really be a poor unhappy lad. Yet I had no other trouble to surmount. The only one I thought the hardest was that father would give me no pocket money.

Mother had been dead six years, when father died of apoplexy in the first month of the year. In April, I graduated from a certain private middle school, and in July, brother from a commercial college. He was offered a position at the Kyushu branch of a certain business concern in Tokyo, and had to go to the South. I had to stay and study more in the capital. Brother said he would sell the house with all the movables belonging to him and go to Kyushu. I told him to do what he thought best. I wished to be entirely independent of him. If he rendered me some assistance, he would surely withdraw it soon, as I should certainly pick a quarrel with him before very long. My head I thought was too precious to bow before such a brother by receiving some trivial help. I thought I could support myself even by being a milkman. In a few days my brother called in some secondhand furniture dealer and disposed of, for almost nothing, all the old and worn-out articles handed down from our ancestors. The house with the grounds was sold to a certain wealthy family through the offices of a certain person. By this, brother seemed to have got quite a handsome sum of money, but of course I did not know the details.

I had moved a month before and had been living in a boarding house at Ogawa-machi, Kanda, until my future career should be settled. Kiyo was very sorry to find that the house she had lived in so many years was to be delivered up to the hands of another person, but she could do nothing as it was not her own. "If you were a little older, you could be heir to the estate," she had repeatedly been saying to me. Could I have been heir by being a little older, there could be no reason why I should be unable to be one now. The poor old woman believed out of her ignorance that greater age could secure one the estate of one's elder brother.

Thus we parted, brother and I. But I did not know what to do with Kiyo. Where could she go? Brother was not in a position to take her to Kyushu, and she would have rejected the idea of being taken so far away, following at his heels. Nor was I able to take care of her then; I was an occupant of a four-and-a-half mat room in a poor boardinghouse, and I would have to evacuate even that whenever necessity demanded. Being at my wits' end, I asked her if she was going to find a new master to serve. She then gave me a final answer by saying that she would be obliged to go and stay with her nephew until I got married and set up a new home. Her nephew was a clerk in a certain law court and was free from leading a hand-to-mouth life. Kiyo had been told two or three times that she could come and stay with him if she would. The invitation had been declined each time on the ground that she preferred the family whom she had so long served and felt quite at home. However, circumstances now seemed to compel her to go to her nephew's as she thought it would be unwise and imprudent for her to serve in a new family, where she would surely have hard experiences again. Still she told me to get married soon and have a new home where she could come and be housekeeper. To this faithful woman, I, who had no blood relationship, was much dearer than her own kin.

Two days before he set out for Kyushu, brother came where I boarded, and gave me six hundred yen, telling me I could either invest that money in some commercial enterprise, or my education. He added that I could spend it any way I pleased, but he would never be responsible for any further assistance. Brother looked taller and nobler to me then. I thought I did not care for such a modest sum of money, yet his unusually simple and frank manner pleased me so much that I accepted it with thanks. He also handed me fifty yen to be given to Kiyo when I saw her, and I received it gladly. Two days later, I saw him off at Shimbashi station, and have never seen him since.

My room was the place where I considered how to spend the six hundred yen. Business was not to my taste and I should certainly fail. Moreover, six hundred yen was too small a sum of money to run a prosperous business. Even if I could have a prosperous business, I would be the loser in the long run, as I might be unable to tell people that I had received a liberal education as my schooling ended with that of a middle school. I said to myself that I did not care a bit for mercantile success; I would rather study with the money at my disposal. Dividing it into three parts, I could use two hundred yen a year, and attend school for three years. I could be something if I worked hard for so long. Then I thought which school was the best for me. I knew that I was not born to be a scholar; especially I had a strong aversion to foreign languages and literature. Even a couple of verses in a twenty-line poem of the so-called new school was entirely jargon to me. Any branch of study I thought would do for me who had a natural dislike to all kinds of learning. Happening to pass by the gate of the Butsuri Gakkō (a special school for the study of physics and mathematics), I noticed an advertisement inviting new students to come. I went in, got a copy of the school directory, and lost no time in going through the details of entrance, believing that I had been led there by some invisible hand. Now it seems to me that this was another mistake caused by that hereditary thoughtlessness.

I worked pretty hard for three years, but having no special gift for study, I always found myself at the end of the class. Time is, however, a mysterious worker, and three years' time made me possessor of a diploma at last. I thought it strange, but finding no particular complaint to make, I made up my mind to keep the certificate like a good boy.

Eight days after my graduation, the principal of the college sent for me. I was asked if I would go as a teacher of mathematics with a salary of forty yen per month to a certain middle school in Shikoku. It is true that I had spent three long years in learning, yet had no intention of being a teacher, or going into the country. However, indecision is what I dislike most, and I answered on the spot that I would accept the offer. This of course came partly from the lack of positions in view, except that of teacher, but the hereditary rashness was again at the bottom of the mistake.

Going was what I should do now that I had promised to go. The four-and-a-half mat room during those three years was my castle where I had neither scolding nor quarrel. It was the time in my life when I felt comparatively at ease but now I had to part with the dear old nest which had given me shelter and protection so long. I had never left Tokyo since I was born save the time of my visit to Kamakura with my classmates. Compared with the place I had to go to now, Kamakura was simply next door. The map showed me the place; it was so small a place as to appear just like the point of a needle. It must certainly be a poor miserable place. What the town was like, or what sort of people lived in it, was entirely unknown to me; yet it gave me neither trouble nor anxiety. The only thing I had to do now was simply to go, and it was a little bit troublesome. That was all.

I often visited Kiyo after we had closed our house. Her nephew was a comparatively good man. He used to entertain me in more ways than one each time I called when he was at home. Kiyo was happy to have me come, and would tell him many fine things about me. Once she declared that I would purchase a fine residence somewhere in Kōjimachi and attend my office in a fine carriage. Being her own judge, she would talk on and on without consulting me, and thus I blushed often, being very much embarrassed. I bore this once or twice like a saint, but found it very hard to bear when she began to spin a yarn how I urinated in my sleep when a child. I do not know how her nephew felt about her proud talk of me, but Kiyo being a woman of the old school thought that her relation to me was that of a vassal to his lord at feudal times, and it was not at all strange logic for her to conclude that her nephew came under the same code. Poor, poor nephew!

The terms had been all settled, and I was to set out for my new school in three days, when I called on Kiyo. She had a cold and was lying in bed in the three-mat room facing north. No sooner had she turned out of her bed on seeing me than she asked me if I was going to have a home pretty soon, still calling me by the fond name of "botchan" (boy-master). She seemed to believe that money would naturally come to one's pocket so soon as one got a diploma. For all the great things she said of me, she still called me by that name. Her excessive love for me seemed to have made her blind to my faults. I simply said to her that I should have no home for the time being, and that I was going into the country in a day or two. She seemed greatly disappointed at hearing this, and began to stroke the gray hair on her temples as if in great perplexity. I felt very sorry and tried to revive her spirits a little by saying to her, "Kiyo, I have to go now, but shall be back soon. You may be quite sure to have me again next summer vacation." These consoling words had very little effect upon her, who appeared just as much disappointed as before. "What shall I buy you for a souvenir? What do you want?" Upon this, she said she should like to have the *sasa-ame* of Echigo. I had never heard of such a cake as that before. Moreover, the place where I was to go was in as different a direction from Echigo as the North Pole is from the South Pole. "I am afraid there seems to be no such thing as *sasa-ame* in the country place where I am to go," said I to her. "In what direction is it situated then?" she asked me again. "The west," was my simple answer. "Is it that or this side of Hakone?" was her next question. The questions and answers of the like just mentioned put me all but out of patience.

Kiyo came very early on the morning of my departure, and did everything she could to help me start properly. She put into my carpet bag some tooth powder, a toothbrush, and a towel which she had bought at some milliner's on the way. I told her that I did not need them, but she would give no ear to what I said. We went down to the station in rickshas. We came out together onto the platform. I got into the carriage and was looking out of the window waiting for the signal, when Kiyo looked up into my face and said in a small, almost inaudible, voice. "This may be the last. Fare you well, my young master." Her eyes were filled with tears. I did not cry, though tears would come out in spite of me. The locomotive began to move with its usual puff, puff. Thinking it quite safe now, I looked out of the window and turned to the spot where she had been standing. There she still stood, looking after me with a longing eye. She appeared so very small.

Chapter 2

No sooner had the steamer stopped with its usual "booh" from its whistle than a boat from the shore came approaching the vessel to receive passengers. The boatman had only a yard of red cloth around his loins; he was as naked as the savages down in the South Sea Islands. Nobody, however, could wear clothes on such a warm day. The sun was pouring down its hot rays upon the water so unpleasantly bright as to make one giddy. I asked the purser if I was to get off here and was told that I was. It was a small fishing village just like Ohmori. A fool I surely was to have been sent so far down to such a miserable place, where no human being could comfortably stay even a day. This was the prevailing thought then; still I could not help it. I quickly jumped into the boat before anybody got in; several followed me. Taking on some half a dozen boxes besides passengers, the boatman with the red loin cloth headed the vessel out to sea. On landing, I was the first to get out. Getting hold of a dirty-nosed urchin standing on the beach, I asked him where the middle school stood. The boy, being taken aback by the abrupt manner of my question, timidly replied, "I do not know." What a poor, dull rustic! not to know where the middle school was in a town so small as the forehead of a cat. Then came a strange-looking man with tight sleeves, who told me to

follow him. Minatoya, or a hotel of some such name, was where
I was taken by the man. Such a volley of welcomes came from
the lips of those disagreeable women in the hotel that I dared
not enter it. I remained standing by the gate. "Two *ri* from here
by train, sir" on my asking where the middle school stood made
me still more inclined not to come in. Taking my two carpet
bags by force from the man with tight sleeves I deliberately
began to walk away to the station. The landlady and her maids
were dumbfounded by this act of mine.

The station was soon reached; the ticket was also bought
easily. The carriage I got in was so small that it looked just like
a match box. The train went rolling on about five minutes or so,
then I had to get off. I had thought it rather strange that the fare
was so small, only three sen. Now it became all clear to me. A
short ride in a ricksha brought me to the middle school where
I found nobody in, as it had already broken up. The janitor told
me that the teacher on night watch was out for a few minutes
on some private errand. What an example of loose discipline,
thought I. Then I thought I might call upon the principal, but
being completely tired out, I got in the ricksha again and told
the puller to take me to any hotel he thought best. The man
gladly took me to a hotel named Yamashiroya, which I thought
a bit interesting. It bore the same name as that of the pawnbroker, Kantaro's father's.

An uninviting dark room just below the staircase was where
I was shown into. It was so close and hot a room, like an oven,
that I told them to let me have some other room. They said
that it was the only room then available, every other room
being unfortunately occupied. Thus I was left alone with my
bags to perspire in the hot room. Patience was what I had to
learn there. Being told to take a bath, I went, jumped in with a
good deal of splash, and came out of the tub in a twinkling. I

noticed on my way back that many a cool, cozy room was left unoccupied. Impudent rascals! They had basely deceived me. Supper was brought in by a maid. The room was hot and uncomfortable, yet the meal was far nicer than that of the boardinghouse in Tokyo. The maid who waited on me was garrulous and asked me where I came from. "From Tokyo," I answered. To the question, "Tokyo is a fine place, is it not?" "There is no doubt about it," was the answer I gave. A great roar of laughter was heard away in the kitchen when the maid carrying away the table things reached there. Thinking the bed was the only place to while away such a dull time, I immediately went to bed and tried to sleep, but sleep I could not. It was not only hot and sultry, but also so clamorous that I thought it five times as noisy as in the boardinghouse. I was dozing over my pillow, when Kiyo, the servant, appeared before me. She was nibbling away at a bamboo leaf with *ame*. I told her that the leaf was not good for her stomach and she had better stop but she kept on eating as if it were a delicacy, saying it was a very good panacea. I was completely taken aback and began to laugh. "Aha, ha" from my outstretched lips awoke me from the state of drowsiness. It was a dream. The maid was taking down the shutters. The sun had risen considerably high and the sky was as clear as could be.

I had been told that you should give a tip when out traveling; that you would never be welcome, without giving a money present on your putting up at a hotel. That I was put into a small dark room could only be accounted for by the fact that I had given them no tip; that I had on shabby clothes, and was carrying old carpet bags and a cheap umbrella. "They have assumingly looked down upon me, these detestable rustics! They shall know how they should behave toward their guests. They shall have a great surprise by being given an enormous tip. Poor as I may look, I brought with me on leaving Tokyo the balance left after paying my school expenses, the handsome sum of thirty yen. After I having paid for train, steamer, and all other miscellaneous expenses on the way I still have fourteen yen left over," said I to myself. "I do not mind if I give away all I have, for I shall get a salary from now on. A gift of five yen will certainly dazzle these miserly rustics. A few moments and a miracle will be wrought." I kept myself cool and quiet. I had washed my face and been waiting in my room a few moments, when the maid (the same maid) brought in my breakfast. Her unpleasant smile at me while serving made me so irritated that I all but flung the rice bowl at the impertinent domestic. "Don't stare me in the face; there is no parade there. Mine is far superior to yours," said I to myself. I planned to give it after I had finished my meal, but too greatly displeased to wait any longer, I took out a five yen bill and told her to take it to the landlord behind the counter. The maid made a very strange face at this act. I went to school after I breakfasted. The shoes had not been polished.

The school was soon reached after I had turned two or three corners, as my ricksha ride on the previous day had made me pretty familiar with the whereabouts of the schoolhouse. Now I found myself just in front of the school gate, where a pavement of granite began until it reached the porch. The unusually big sound my ricksha made on the pavement yesterday I remember bothered me not a little. I met on my way many students in thick cotton cloth uniform, who all passed into the gate. Some of them were much taller and looked much stronger than I. I felt somewhat uneasy when I thought I had to teach those rustic lads. Sending in my card, I was shown into the room of the principal, who looked just like a badger, with a thin moustache, a dark complexion, and big eyes. His haughty manner was anything but pleasing. An official writ with a large stamp was ceremoniously handed to me with the words, "Please be faithful and diligent in your duty," from the dignified head of the school. This very writ was by-the-by rolled up and thrown overboard on my way back to Tokyo. Then the principal told me that I should be introduced to the teachers immediately; that I should show the document to each of them. This was decidedly an example of red tapism. It would have been far better to paste it up on the wall of the teachers' room for three days than to make one go through such a troublesome process.

There was much time to wait before the teachers all assembled in the teachers' room at the trumpet call at the end of the first period. Then the principal, looking at his watch, said that he would tell me all the principal points I should bear in mind, though the details would be gradually unfolded. He then dwelt upon the spirit and importance of true education, giving full scope to his pedagogical knowledge. I had of course been paying lukewarm attention to what he was saying, and while listening I began to wish that I had not come to such a place. It was impossible for me to do just as the principal wished me to do. Taking hold of one so quick tempered as a bullet, he said, "Be an example to the boys; try to be looked up to as a living virtue of the school. The true enducator is he who, besides his learning, will impart his personal influence over his pupils, etc., etc." These were exorbitant expectations from one like myself. Forty yen a month would have been too small an allurement for one so great as the principal mentioned to come so far down to such a wretched country place. I thought that human nature is the same all over the world, so that everybody would fall out once or twice when angry. If such was the case, silence seemed here to be the only virtue to keep me safe. The principal should have told me before all the details of duties I should perform. I could not tell him that I would do all he had told me, for it would have been a sheer lie. I had been deceived and come here;

fate was at the bottom of the whole affair, and the only thing that remained for me now was to act like a man, and go back to Tokyo resigning on the spot. I had given the landlord five yen and the balance in my purse was only nine yen and some old coins. Nine yen would not be sufficient to take me back to Tokyo. Would that I had not given that tip! Though the money was not enough, yet I might be able to manage it. Thinking that lack of traveling expenses would be far better than to be dishonest, I frankly said to him. "Mr. Principal, I can hardly do as you wish me to do. Please take this official writ." At this, the astonished principal stared me in the face with his badgerlike eyes for some moments and then told me that those were simply wishes, fulfillment of which would be hard for anybody, and that I need not worry about it. Thus saying, he laughed outright. Had he understood the ways of the world so well, why did he threaten me with impossibilities, I wonder?

In the meantime came the bugle call. All at once a buzzing sound like that of a beehive was heard toward the classrooms. Upon the intimation that the teachers had all assembled, I went into the teachers' room, the principal going before me. It was a large oblong room with desks around, at which teachers sat. On my entering the room, they one and all looked at me as if I were an animal on show. Then followed the ceremony of bowing with appropriate words. I approached and showed the official writ to each of the teachers, most of whom, leaving their seats, simply curved their bodies a little in recognition. Politer ones, however, receiving the document from me gave it a careful glance and returned it to me with a profound bow. I thought it just like a stage performance in the country theater. I had repeated this same act fourteen times; and, when I came to the teacher of physical exercise for the fifteenth, I felt a little impatient. As to the teachers, they had to do it once, but I had to go through the same process fifteen times. They should have been more considerate and sympathetic.

Dean So-and-so, *bungakushi*, was among those whom I greeted. A *bungakushi*, being a graduate of the Imperial University, must be, I thought, a great savant. He had the sweet caressing voice a lady would be proud of being possessor. One thing that gave me the greatest surprise was that he had on a flannel shirt on such a warm day. Though it was of a thinner kind of cloth, it must be quite warm. Elaborate toilet must be inseparable to a *bungakushi*, I thought; and when you saw it was a red shirt you could not but be dumbfounded. I was told afterwards that he had on nothing but a red shirt all through the twelve months. A strange fancy! Was not his explanation funny? He said that red being good for health, he always got red underwear made. Then why did he not get red trousers as well? A teacher of English, named Koga, was another figure whom we cannot pass by without some comment. He had a very sickly complexion. A man of pale face is generally thin and lank, but he was exceptionally pale and stout. I remember, when a school boy, I had a classmate named Asai, whose father was a farmer, and he had a complexion just like that of this professor of English. Once I asked Kiyo if a farmer always had such a pale face and she told me that was not the case, but it was because he was eating nothing but green squash. Since then, whenever I saw a man of wan face, I firmly believed that it was the result of his having had green squash. This teacher of English must have taken a good deal of green squash. Even now I am not a bit wiser about that squash affair. I asked Kiyo to explain what it was, but she simply smiled and gave me no answer. I dare say she did not know what it was herself. Hotta was the name of a teacher of mathematics. He had a round head cropped short, and it was just like a chestnut burr. He had such a bad physiognomy as that of a bad priest of *Eizan* (the

site of a famous Buddhist temple on the top of Mt. Hiei, Kyoto).
Giving not a single glance, even when the writ was shown him,
he simply said, "You are the new teacher? Come to see me." He
closed his remark with "Ha, ha." What did he mean by his "Ha,
ha's"? Nobody would go and see such a savage. Porcupine was the
nickname I gave this chestnut burr, and thought it very appropriate. The teacher of Chinese Classics was very polite as a man
of the school should be. "You arrived yesterday? Must be very
tired; are you going to begin your work right away? What an example of diligence!" He went on talking without waiting for my
answer. An amiable old man, thought I. The teacher of drawing
was a man of the stage professional type. He had on a summer
haori made of thin silklike tissue paper. Opening and shutting
his fan, he asked me where I came from. "Eh, from Tokyo?" said
he; "I am so glad to hear it. You and I then are both Yedo men."
If such a person were a Yedo man, I thought, nobody would like
to have been born in Tokyo. Were I to write such things of them
in detail, it would require a volume. I had best stop.

The introduction being now over, the principal told me that
I might go home and have a conference about my class work
with the chief instructor of mathematics afterward; and then I
should meet the classes the day after tomorrow. Our Porcupine
was found to be the principal teacher of mathematics. The revelation was anything but pleasant; I was not a little disappointed
to know that I had to work under him. "Say, where are you staying? Yamashiroya? Well, I'll come and have a talk with you this
afternoon." With these words, Porcupine left me and went away
to his class with a chalk box. What a humble teacher he was,
who would come and see his inferior personally instead of sum-
moning him. Still it was a good act on the part of Mr. Porcupine.

Coming out of the school gate, I should have gone back to
my hotel, but knowing there was no special attraction there I

thought I would take a look at the town and walked on and on along the streets just as chance took me. I saw the building of the prefectural government; it was an old edifice of the last century. I saw the barracks; they were not so nice as those of the Azabu Regiment. I passed the main street, and it was not half so wide as Kagurazaka and with much poorer shops. The castle town of 250,000 *koku* was only great in name. The people who were proudly calling it by the high-sounding appellation of "castle town" were rather to be pitied than to be envied. While walking with some such thoughts, I found myself just in front of Yamashiroya, the hotel. I expected the town was much larger, but it was so small that there was nothing more to see. I had scarcely entered the gate when the hostess at the counter came out quickly and welcomed me with sweet words bowing so very low that her head almost reached the floor. Taking off my shoes, I went in and was shown into a room by the maid; she said it had just been evacuated. It was a fifteen mat front room upstairs with a large fine *tokonoma*. I had never been in such a fine parlor before and being very doubtful whether I should ever be able to live in such a splendid room again in my whole life, I took off my foreign clothes, put on *yukata*, and lay on my back in the midst of the room giving full freedom to my liberated limbs. It was so very delightful.

After the midday meal I lost no time in writing to my Kiyo. Letter-writing is what I dislike most, for I am neither good at composition nor rich in vocabulary. Moreover, I have no special person to write to. However, Kiyo would certainly be in great anxiety and might be thinking that I had been drowned in a shipwreck. In order to make her believe that her fear and anxiety were entirely unfounded, I wrote her a very long letter. It was worded as follows:

Dear Kiyo,

I got here only yesterday. It is a poor place. I am lying down in a large room of fifteen mats. I gave away five yen as tip. The landlady made me the nicest bow you ever saw; her head all but touched the floor. I had a disturbed sleep last night; had a dream in which you ate *sasa-ame,* bamboo leaf and all. Expect me next summer vacation. I have been to school today and many of the teachers have been given nicknames by me. Principal, Badger; dean, Red-shirt; teacher of English, Green Squash; teacher of mathematics, Porcupine; teacher of drawing, Clown. You shall know many more things by-and-by. Good-by, Kiyo.

Yours,
B.

I felt so light of heart and drowsy after I had finished the letter to Kiyo that I laid myself down in the middle of the room with my limbs all outstretched. This time no dream came to disturb my profound sleep. "Is this the room you are in?" coming from somebody in a loud voice awoke me and my sleepy eyes rested on no other person than Mr. Porcupine himself. No sooner had I sprung up than he, with an inserted clause of apology about his disrespectful behavior toward me at our last interview at school that morning, began to talk about the books and the number of hours I had to teach. I was not a little perplexed at his abrupt way of business. I told him I would attend to the duties, as I found them not so very hard. If such were the duties, I should never have been a bit surprised if I had been told to begin right away instead of waiting till the day after tomorrow. The consultation was of brief duration. Mr. Porcupine then said that he presumed I did not intend to stay in that hotel any longer and would be glad to move quickly if he found a good boarding place for me; that no other person could persuade them to take in a boarder, but he could; that I should come and see the place myself that very day, move in the next day, and attend school the day after. He seemed to settle every thing according to his own convenience and satisfaction, not caring a pin for me. However, no sensible man would have thought of staying in a fifteen mat room much longer. All my salary would not be enough to pay my hotel bill. Although I did not think it nice to move out so soon now that I had given them five yen as a tip, yet if I moved at all it would be far better to do it right away and be settled once and for all. Thus thinking, I asked Mr. Porcupine to do it for me. I went with him as he told me to come and see. The house stood on a hill side at the outskirt of the town and it was a very quiet place. The master of the house named Ikagin was a dealer in curios, whose wife, an elderly woman, was four years older than her husband. I remember I learned, while attending the middle school, the word "witch." The features of this woman were so much like those of a witch; yet witch or not was no business of mine as long as she was another's wife. Everything being now settled to the satisfaction of both parties, the curio dealer and his wife said they would expect me the following day. On our way home, Mr. Porcupine treated me to a glass of ice water at a shop on the street. When I saw him at school, he seemed so disagreeably haughty and impolite, but seeing these kind offices he was so willing to offer me, I could not but be persuaded that he was good at heart. The similarity of character between him and me was so very striking; he was as hasty, driving, and quick tempered as I. His great popularity, however, was partly due to this weakness of character, if it be weakness at all.

Chapter 3

At last the day arrived on which I went to school. I felt very awkward when, entering the classroom, I got up on the platform for the first time. I began to feel the doubt, while teaching, whether I could ever be a good teacher. There was a stir and commotion among the boys. Now and again came a surprisingly loud voice calling out "Master." This address of "master" made me not a little uncomfortable. I used, it is true, to call out "master, master" every day while I was attending the Physics College, but to be addressed "master" was quite another matter and sent a tickling sensation all through my system even so far down as the soles of my feet. I am neither coward nor dastard, yet, sad to say, I lack coolness. Hearing "master" in a loud voice made me feel as if I heard the midday gun on the Palace grounds when hungry. The first hour I spent as best as I could. I was pestered with no specially hard questions to answer. Coming back to the faculty room, I was asked by Mr. Porcupine if it had been all right. The brief answer, "Oh, yes," seemed to have given him ample satisfaction.

Going with a chalk box to the classroom from the teachers' room at the second hour gave me a feeling as if I were riding into a hostile land. Entering the room, I found that it was composed of lads much bigger than those in the other room. Being a Yedo man of small and delicate build, I could not make a commanding figure even on an elevated platform. I would not shrink from fighting a wrestler if opportunity demanded so doing, but I have neither skill nor art to intimidate with an exercise of the tongue those big boys, forty in number. However, it would not do to show it by any means, and I began my lecture in a very loud voice, giving a slight twist to my tongue. At first, the boys did not know what to do; they were, so to speak, groping in a dense smoke, and this made me so much bolder and more triumphant that I went on talking much faster, freely using slang expressions. All at once came "master" from the biggest and strongest boy, who stood up in the middle of the front row. "What is it?" said I to him in a tone as if I had long expected it. "Sir, you talk too fast to follow. Will you not, if you please speak a little more slowly?" "Will you not, if you please?" is a hatefully moderate expression. "I'll oblige you by speaking more slowly if you really cannot follow me," said I. "But being a Yedo man through and through, I cannot speak your dreadful dialect, and you'll have to wait patiently until you can understand me." Thus the second period passed much more peacefully than had been expected. Cold perspiration, however, seemed to cover my whole system, when one of the lads approached me with a hard problem of Euclid, saying, "Will you not solve this for me, if you please?" One glance showed me that it was beyond my power to explain it. Finding no better way than to say frankly that I could hardly make out what it was, and that he should learn it some other time, I beat a hasty retreat. A volley of shouts mixed with "Whew, poor teacher," was sent after me. Rascals! A teacher is as human as they. Being human, it is no wonder if he does not know everything and says so honestly. Nobody would come so far down to such a country place with such a small salary as forty yen, if he were able to explain such a hard question.

Saying this to myself, I came back to the faculty room. "How has it been this time?" said Mr. Porcupine. "Well," I answered, but the simple interjection giving me no satisfaction, I told him that the students there in the school were all fools. Mr. Porcupine made a face at this remark.

The third, the fourth periods in the forenoon and the first period in the afternoon passed without much difference. My first day at school was, however, not a success, but a day of little failures. I thought the teacher's vocation was not so easy as outsiders think. Teaching was now over, yet I could not go home; I had to wait till three although I had nothing more to do. Three o'clock, and I was to go and inspect the classrooms upon receiving word that they had been swept and cleaned by the boys under my personal charge. I was not yet free until I had done one more duty, that is—looking over the roll calls. Though a salary-drawing creature, yet I thought it a cruel law that bound one to school, and made him stare at his desk even when he had no class to teach. But as other teachers were attending to their duties like good boys, I patiently waited, thinking it would not do for a newcomer like myself to fret. On our way home, however, I said to Mr. Porcupine that it was foolishness itself to compel one to stay in school till three willingly or unwillingly. This complaint drew from him his usual "Well, yes, aha, ha!" But soon it changed into a grave tone. "Do not speak so ill of the school. Be on your guard, lest some ill-disposed persons should betray you. Speak to me only if you have to do it at all," said he in as much a form of warning as friendly advice. As we parted at the next corner, I had no time to inquire into the details. Getting home, I was called on by the master of the house where I boarded with the words, "Shall I make tea, sir?" I understood from the tone that he would entertain me with the tea made from the leaves of his own can, but it was not the case; he took and made tea from my can and freely helped himself to the beverage. I suspected from this that he had been helping himself to it as he pleased while I was away from home. The master said, "Being excessively fond of old paintings and curios, I have at last come to be privately engaged in this business. You seem to have elegant taste, and what would you say if I advise you to amuse yourself a little with curios just for recreation's sake?" This was to me entirely a bit of unexpected solicitation. It is true that I had been taken for a lock mender when I went to the Imperial Hotel on an errand, and that ricksha pullers addressed me as "Leader" when with a blanket on I visited the Great Buddha at Kamakura. I have been up to this time mistaken for many other things, but never have I met with any one who said I was a man of elegant taste. One's dress or appearance generally betrays what he is. A man of fine taste will have on a fancy hood, carrying in his hand a narrow slip of paper called tanzaku to write verses on, as he is seen represented in pictures. A man who could placidly say that I had refined taste, I thought, was no novice in imposture. On my telling him that I, not being an old man in easy retirement, disliked such things, he answered with a smile that nobody was born with such taste, but once obtained he could hardly get rid of it. So saying, he helped himself to the tea he himself had made, handling the cup in a curious way. I had indeed asked the host to buy me some tea last night, but such bitter strong tea would not do; one cup of the beverage he made seemed to contract my stomach. "Please get me some weaker tea." I said to him. "Yes, if it pleases you, sir," was his insinuating answer, and he again helped himself to one more cupful of tea. Thinking it no tax upon his purse, the host took as many cups as he possibly could. After he had gone, I looked over the lessons for the following day and went to bed.

I worked at school day after day as regularly as the sun rises, and coming home was pestered every day by my host with his usual "I'll make tea for you, sir." A week passed, and I was able to understand the general affairs of the school, and the character of both my host and hostess pretty well. My colleagues told me on my asking that from one week to one month after you have got your written appointment you are very anxious whether you have been well or ill received by the students. I had no such anxiety. It is true that I felt rather bad when I blundered in the classroom once and again, but it was of short duration. Thirty minutes or so, and I was again a happy man. I am a man who could never be anxious long about anything if I tried. I was quite indifferent as to how my blunders in class would affect the students, and consequently bring the disfavor of both the principal and the dean upon me. As I said before, I am timid at heart, but am not a man who will look back with his hands on the plough. In case this school did not want me, I was any moment ready to go elsewhere, and was not a bit afraid of either Badger or Red-shirt. And of course I had no mind to say some sweet words or complimentary remarks to the boys in the classroom.

Thus it was all right with the school, but it would not do with the home where I boarded. I could have borne pretty well with the landlord who came and helped himself to the tea from my own can, but he was not content with that. He would bring various things in and tried to make a customer of me. Some dozen ornamental seals were first brought in by him, who asked me to buy them for three yen and said it was a bargain. I told him that I, not being a poor artist going around country places, did not need them. Next time he came in with a hanging scroll of flowers and birds painted by a certain artist named Kwazan. Hanging it himself on the *tokonoma,* he admiringly said to me,

"Is it not a perfect finish?" "Well—yes?" was my equivocal answer. He went on lecturing. "There were two painters who bore the same nom-de-plume, but different family names, and this is a work done by such and such Kwazan." After spinning a long yarn, he urged me to buy it, for he would charge *me* only fifteen yen. I declined the offer on the ground that I had no money with me. Obstinacy seemed to be his characteristic trait. He said that I need not worry about it; that I could pay it any time which suited me best. Frankness was now the only means to drive away this brazen-faced host. "I would not buy such stuff even if I had money" at last succeeded in driving him away. A stone ink slab *(suzuri)* as big as a devil tile (a big ornamental tile) was next brought in. He repeatedly said it was a *tankei*. Wishing to have some fun at his expense, I asked him to explain it to me. He said, "There are upper, middle, and lower layers of stone in the quarry called *Tankei* in China, and ink slabs now on sale in the market are all of the upper layer, but this is surely of the middle one. Look at these 'eyes.' An ink slab with three eyes is a rarity. A rub or two with your ink stick *(sumi)* on the slab will convince you of the truth of my statement. Just try." Thus saying, he pushed the great *suzuri* toward me. "What is its price?" I asked. He told me that the owner, having brought it back from China, wished to dispose of it, and that thirty yen would be quite a reasonable price. This fellow must be a fool, I thought. It seemed that I might be able to get along pretty well with the school, but his bric-a-brac attack would drive me mad before very long.

In the meantime, the school had begun to interest me but little. One evening I was taking a walk along the street named Omachi, when near the post office a sign lantern with the characters *soba* (buckwheat), "Tokyo style" underneath it in the way of a footnote attracted my attention. I am very fond of buckwheat. While in Tokyo, I could hardly resist the temptation to go into the shop through the curtain, when I happened to pass and smelt the high flavor of the seasonings from a buckwheat shop. My mind had been absorbed till now in mathematics and curios, buckwheat having been placed in the background. Now that I saw the familiar signboard inviting me to come in, I could not but follow the call of my palate. I went in, thinking I would treat myself with a bowl or two. The interior of the shop was anything but clean. The signboard did not tell the truth. I wished it had been much cleaner, judging from the conspicuous characters "Tokyo" on the paper lantern. But either from the ignorance of Tokyo, or the want of money on the part of the keeper, the room was extremely dirty. The mats were all discolored with grains of sand. The walls were all black with soot. The ceiling smouldering with the smoke from the petroleum lamp was so very low that you would unconsciously duck. The only thing that was quite new and pasted up in a conspicuous place was the bill of fare with prices written in pompous characters. In all probability, the business was purchased and opened by a new proprietor a few days ago. The first item in the bill was buckwheat with fried fish. "Give me *tempura*," called out in a rather loud voice, caused those who, in the corner of the room, had been helping themselves to soba, eating with a hissing sound, to turn their eyes to me all at one time. As the room was dark, I had not noticed it, but one glance showed me they were all the students of my middle school. I returned them a salutation as they had done me the same. I had not taken *soba* for so long and since it was good, I did ample justice to four bowls of *soba* with *tempura* that evening.

Next morning I went into the classroom without any concern, and found "Prof. Tempura" written in such large letters on the blackboard that they all but covered it. No sooner had the boys seen my face than they burst into uproarious laughter. As it all seemed nonsense, I demanded if it were not right for one to eat *tempura*. Then one of the boys replied that it was all right to eat *tempura*, yet four bowls were too much. I told them that it was not their business at all whether I took four or five bowls with my own money, and giving a lecture in a hurry beat a hasty retreat to the teachers' room. After ten minutes' recess, I went to another class whose blackboard was found to be decorated with the following characters: "Four bowls of *tempura*, but you must not laugh." I was not a bit angry last time, but this time I thought it impertinence itself. Joke when indulged in to excess is no longer joke, but mischief. It is something like baked *mochi* done too much, which nobody will take the trouble to eat. It may be that the country people, not knowing how far to go and where to stop, think it all right to push it as far as they possibly can. Their castle town is so small an affair that an hour's sight seeing will bring you to an end of everything it contains, and as they had no other accomplishment to pride themselves upon they treated the *tempura* business as if it were such a great event as the Russo-Japanese War. Poor, poor souls! As they are brought up from infancy in such a way, it goes without saying that they will grow up to be precocious and crooked like a dwarfed maple tree trained up in a flower pot. I would laugh with them if it were done in a spirit of juvenile innocence. But what was it? Boys should be boys to the marrow, but the act was certainly that of a matured man of poisonous spirit. Quietly rubbing out the characters on the blackboard, I demanded if such mischief had given them satisfaction. An ignoble joke! "Do you know the meaning of the word ignominy?" said I to the boys. Then came a voice saying, "Meanness is the anger shown by one whose act excites laughter." I thought that disagreeable fellow had the best of it. Be that as it may, when I reflected how I had come so far down from Tokyo to teach such savages, my heart began to fail. "Do not talk nonsense but work hard," said I to the boys and began teaching right away. The blackboard of the next classroom saluted me with the following: "Take *tempura* and your organ of speech will get oily and make you talk insolently." I came to catch them, but they had already disappeared from the scene. My patience having been overtaxed, I told them that I would not teach such assuming rascals any more and left the classroom in an angry mood. I was told afterward that the boys were very much pleased, as they had no more work that hour. Things having come to such a state, my landlord's curios seemed to be far more bearable than the school with its detestable ingredients.

However, a good night's sleep over the *tempura* affair arrested my irritability. In the morning, I went to school and found all the boys present. I could hardly make out what it all meant. Nothing worthy of note happened until the fourth day, on the evening of which I visited and ate dumpling at a place named Sumida. This is a town noted for its hot springs, which can be reached from the castle town in ten minutes by rail, and thirty minutes on foot. The hot spring resort has houses of ill fame besides restaurants, hotels, and a park. The dumpling shop at the entrance to the brothel quarters being famous for the sweetness of the bread, I just stepped in on my way home and tasted some. This time meeting no students, I thought nobody had seen me there. Going to school next morning, I went into the classroom and was saluted by the letters, "Two plates of dumpling—seven sen" on the blackboard. It is true that I had taken two plates and paid seven sen. What a nuisance! Fully expecting the second period would bring me again some kind of fresh annoyance, I went to the classroom and found on the board "Dumplings in the brothel quarters are nice, very nice!" I was completely dumbfounded by this act of obstinacy and impertinence. The dumpling affair thus passed away to return no more, but it was soon followed by another. It was nothing but an innocent red towel which excited their curiosity. How did it happen? It simply came to pass in this way. Ever since my arrival here, I had made it a regular habit of going to the hot spring at Sumida everyday. Every other thing made a very poor comparison with things in Tokyo, but as to the hot spring, it was just splendid. As I had taken so much trouble to come so far down, I thought I would go and have a bath there everyday. So I would walk down there in the way of exercise every evening before supper. Whenever I went, I took a large foreign towel, the ends of which were dangling down from my girdle. The mineral water had given it a yellowish tint, and together with the color running out of the red stripe on it, it turned rouge. It was my constant companion going and coming. It was with me in the railway carriage; it was with me when I took a walk. Thus the boys came to call me "Red Towel." How annoying it is to have to live in a small town and be an object of criticism! I have more to tell. A new three-storied house was the bath house where I used to go. If you went first class, you could get a bath robe and wash by the servant as well. Moreover, a pretty maid would serve you tea in a cup called *temmoku*. I always went first class. Then they began to say that it was very extravagant for a teacher whose salary was only forty yen a month to go first class. They had better mind their own business, I should like to say. This is not all. The bath tank was of granite; it was as large as a fifteen-mat room. Generally thirteen or fourteen persons were found bathing in it, but sometimes there were none. The water came up to your breast and it was very nice for one to go in and swim in the tank. But one day as I went downstairs in high spirits from the third floor fully expecting to have a nice swim again that day, I peeped through the narrow wicket into the bath tank and was greeted by a big placard nailed high up with the bold black letters, "No swimming in the tank!" As very few but myself would think of swimming in the tub, this placard must have been specially made to warn me. I took warning and ceased to think of swimming in the tank again. Yes, I gave up the desire like a man. I was, however, not a little confused when, entering the classroom, I saw on the blackboard, "Kindly refrain from swimming in the tub." It seemed as if all the students were spies watching every move and act I made. Dejection came upon me. Let the boys do and say as they will, I am not a man who will give up on account of their interference the plan he has set his heart on. But my heart began to fail me when I thought why I had come down to such a small miserable town where the tip of your nose finds limitation whenever you move about. And home with its curio persecution was no more consolation to me than the school itself.

Chapter 4

Night watch at school is a duty imposed upon each member of the faculty. They take turns in doing it. Principal Badger and Dean Red Shirt were exceptions to the rule. On asking why, I was told that they were freed from the duty, because they were treated as officials of *Sōnin* Rank. Beggarly pretext! They drew large salaries; their hours of teaching were few, yet they were exempted from the duty they should perform. What an example of injustice! An unjust law had been enacted for their own convenience, and they were so shameless as to show innocent faces before men. I wonder how they could be so brazen faced! I was exceedingly indignant at this wrong committed with impunity. Mr. Porcupine was of opinion that whatever complaints one might make, it was of little avail. But it was my firm conviction that justice, even unaided, can carry its point. Mr. Porcupine quoting the English proverb, "Might is Right," gave me a warning, which was far from being satisfactory. I asked him what it meant, and he said it meant "the right of the mighty." If that was all, I had known it long ago, and Mr. Porcupine's explanation could not make me a bit wiser. The right of the mighty and night duty are quite different things, and no sensible man would acquiesce in the statement that Badger and Red-shirt were the mighty. Setting argument aside, however, my turn of keeping night watch came around at last. Being naturally nervous, I could have no sound sleep unless I rested in my bed with bedding of my own. I had seldom stayed overnight at a friend's house since a child. If a friend's home failed to give me a night's rest, how could the cold bed of the dormitory satisfy me? I disliked the duty, yet, if it were included in the salary of forty yen, I thought it could not be helped, and I had better attend to it like a good boy.

Teachers and boys had all gone home. I was left alone to brood over time's slow progress. The room in which I was to keep night watch was situated at the western extremity of the dormitory built in the back part of the classrooms. I just entered and had a look at it. The setting sun was so mercilessly pouring its rays direct upon it that no human being could stay there even a minute. Autumn in the country seemed to take so long in coming, and the Indian summer was intolerably hot. I had a ration of the boys' evening meal brought in and made a hurried supper on it. So distasteful was it that I could not eat half as much as I wished. I wondered how the boys who took such poor food could be so full of life and mischief; and when you are told that they took it as early as half-past four in the afternoon and dispatched it in no time, you will naturally think they were heroes. Supper had I taken, but I could not well go to bed as the sun was not yet gone down. A desire to go to the hot spring had become urgent. I do not know whether it is right or not to go out when one is on night duty; but to be confined like a prisoner in a bare, comfortless room taxed my patience far beyond endurance. When I first came to the school and asked the janitor if the teacher on night watch was in, he said that he was out on business. At the time I thought it strange; now that my turn came around I could not but sympathize with the teacher; he was right in going out. The *ennui* would have killed him. On my telling the servant that I should be gone a while, he asked me if I had some business out. "No," said I "But I am going to the hot spring to have a bath." Thus saying, I went on my way. It was a pity that I had left my red towel behind in the house where I boarded, but one borrowed over there would do for once.

At last evening came after I had gone in and out of the bath tank several times. Taking the train, I got down at the Furumachi station. Only four *cho* from here to the school. Thinking it could be covered in a few minutes, I had gone on several steps, when Badger came in sight. I dare say he had planned to take the train to the hot spring, too. Briskly coming toward me, he gave me a side glance as he passed. I made him a slight bow in recognition. "Well," said he in a serious tone, "you are on night duty this evening, are you not?" His "are you not?" irritated me not a little. Was it not only two hours ago that he thanked me saying, "You are on duty tonight. You have never been on before. I thank you for the trouble." It never occurred to me that so soon as one became principal one should have to use such a roundabout expression. Being much offended, I told him bluntly that I knew I was on duty that night and was on my way to school to perform my assigned duty. Thus saying, I strutted away from him in a slow, unconcerned way. Hardly had I reached the turning of Tate street when Mr. Porcupine was in front of me. What a small place it is! You go out and you are quite sure to meet somebody of your acquaintance. "Are you not on night watch?" said he to me. "Yes, I am," I answered. "If so, it is wrong for you to be out." "Nothing wrong," I replied; "it is wrong not to be out." This boastful answer drew another remark from him. "Away with your independence. Don't you know you will have a hard time of it if you meet the principal or the dean?" This admonition was something unusual with Mr. Porcupine. "Well," said I, "I met the principal just now, and he thanked me saying, that it was very hard to be on night watch on such a sultry night, and that I had best be out for a walk." With this, I briskly walked away from him toward school, wishing to have no more trouble with him.

Evening soon came with its black veil. The janitor had been called into the room where I was to keep night watch, and we gossiped away about two hours after dark. The talk having lost its novelty, I thought I would go to bed, though sleep might be slow in coming. I undressed, put on the nightgown, rolled up the mosquito net, lifted up the red blanket and, dropping on my buttocks on the bed with a slight thud, I laid myself down on my back. The action last mentioned has been my habit ever since I was a child. Once I remember that while staying in a boardinghouse in Ogawamachi, a student of a certain law school, an occupant of an upstairs room, came and complained to me saying it was a very bad habit. A law student is very clever at speech, though cowardly at heart, and this one began to spin a long yarn. I let him have his say and composedly told him to his discomfiture that it was not the fault of my rump, but the fault lay in the poor structure of the boardinghouse, which made such a disagreeable sound whenever one got about, and that he had better go and make complaints to the landlord himself. I had no such fear in this chamber in laying myself down with a thud, as the room was downstairs. I lay down as energetically as I could, for I do not feel quite rested unless I do so. Scarcely had I stretched my legs with a pleasurable feeling than something crawled on my leg. I was sure that it was not a flea as it was rather rough when I felt it. What was it then? Extreme alarm made me shake the leg in the blanket. The shaking drove out so many more disagreeable things, rough to the touch. Five or six came onto my shin; two or three on my thigh; one was smashed under my rump; another was bold enough to come so

"You wretched miserable grasshoppers! You have dared to frighten
me. Retaliation you shall have."

far up as the navel. Helter-skelter! getting up in lightning speed, I took out and threw the blanket to the bottom of the bed. This maneuver drew out some fifty or sixty grasshoppers from the bed cover. It is true that I had fear, more or less, before the true character of the things came to light, but now that grasshoppers were found to have been the cause of my alarm, I could not but be offended. Thus saying, I took up the pillow with case and all, and flung it at the poor insects two or three times. This act did not bring forth the expected result, as the targets of my blows were too small. Finding no better way, I sat down on the bed, and rolling up a mat as it is done at the time of "soot cleaning," I began to beat the *tatami* aimlessly and recklessly. The grasshoppers were greatly terrified, but being caught up into the air by incessant motions of the pillow they flew about in every direction. Some of them boldly came and took hold of my shoulders, and my head and the tip of my nose; others were arrogant enough to strike against me in passing. Those that had perched on my head were spared the blow of the pillow, as it would hardly do for me to drive them away with it. Seizing them with my hand, I flung them away with all my might, but what taxed my patience most was that, however hard I might throw them away, it brought no apparent effect, as the insects would gently get hold of the net, only giving it a slight curve. The grasshoppers, far from dying, looked as innocent and calm on the net as if a severe wind storm had just passed over. The engagement lasted about thirty minutes, before all the poor insects were put to death. I got the broom and swept the carcasses all out of the room. The janitor appeared and asked me what the matter was. "Away with your 'what's the matter?' No sensible person would think of keeping grasshoppers in his bed. You blockhead!" At these bitter words of anger, the school servant apologized to me saying that he knew nothing about it. Much offended at his poor excuse, I hurled the broom at the janitor in the veranda, who in great astonishment picked it up and carried it away on his shoulder.

I lost no time in calling in some three of the boarding students to represent the whole dormitory. Then half a dozen made their appearance. I did not care a pin whether a dozen or half a dozen came. Rolling up the sleeve of my nightgown to show my determination, I began interrogations.

"How dare you put grasshoppers in my bed?" said I.

"What is a grasshopper?" asked one of those who sat in front. He was so self-possessed that it approached impertinence. It seemed to me that not only the principal but also the boys of this school were crooked and sophistical in their speech.

"You do not know a grasshopper? You shall see it now." But happening to have no grasshoppers on hand, as I had swept them all away, I called in the janitor again and told him to bring the insects he had put away. He said that they had already been cast away into the dirt hole, and asked me if he was to bring them to me again. I told him that he should, and should do it at once. He ran out of the room and pretty soon bringing back some dozen grasshoppers on a sheet of paper, he apologizingly said, "I am so sorry; but because of the darkness of the night these are all I could gather: you shall have more tomorrow, sir." The lack of sense seemed here to pervade all down to the janitor himself. I picked up one of the insects and showing it to the boys said, "This is a grasshopper. You should be ashamed of your big bodies if you do not know the grasshopper." At this, a fellow with a round face who sat at the extreme left said, "Why, it's a locust, don't you see?" and he looked so wise over the victory. "You fool!" retorted I. "A locust and a grasshopper are the same, only different in name. Moreover, 'don't you see?' is an extremely impolite expression to your teacher. What is your

Namoshi? *Nameshi* is eaten only when you take *dengaku*." At this rebuff, he said that *Namoshi* and *Nameshi* are not the same. This fellow would not give up his dreadful *Namoshi** to the last.

"Locusts or grasshoppers, you can take your choice, but how dared you put them in my bed? When did I ask you to put them?"

"Why, nobody did."

"How could I find them in my bed if you had not put them in?"

"Well, locusts are fond of a warm place, and naturally they found their way into your bed."

"Away with your nonsense! How could you say grasshoppers crept in by themselves?—There can be no bearing with grasshoppers in one's bed.—Why did you play such a bad trick? Confess, quickly."

"Well, but we never did. How can we confess that which we have never done?"

"Cowards! If you cannot confess what you have actually done you should never have done it. Be there no evidence against you, you think yourself quite safe, boldly putting on an innocent face. Even I, while in middle school, did play a few tricks. But when asked who had done the tricks, I was never so base and mean as to shrink back from the responsibility. What's done is done. What's not done is not done. I have been, it is true, the perpetrator of many a naughty thing, but have always been honest and frank. I would never play a trick if I were to escape punishment by telling a lie. Mischief and punishment are inseparable. The very existence of chastisement gives a trick a seasoning as attractive and enticing as a siren. No country under the sun will tolerate a man so mean and base as to try to

---

* Here is a play on words, *namoshi and nameshi*. It is entirely beyond my power to render them into appropriate English.

escape the consequences of crimes he has perpetrated. Money he would borrow, but never think of repaying. Such a rascal will naturally come out of such a school as this. What kind of schooling in the world are they receiving in this middle school? They come to school, tell lies, deceive others, play many bad tricks as stealthily as mice, and when they are graduated, they strut about the world like peacocks. Were true education as such, it would not be a blessing, but rather a curse. You wretched bums!"

I thought it was simply a waste of time to talk to such worthless, rotten-spirited fellows. "Well, if you cannot, or will not, confess what you have actually done, you need not do so, and you may go." Thus I dismissed the boys. I am refined neither in speech nor in manner. But I thought I had a good heart—a heart much nobler than that of those cowardly lads. The six boys left me and went on their way placidly and composedly as if they thought they were much superior to their teacher. However, their self-possessed manner itself betrayed their evil disposition. I could never put on such boldness even if I tried.

Hardly had I got into bed and laid myself down again, when I found the net was full of buzzing mosquitoes. They had probably found their way into the net during the disturbance. However, it would never do to burn the poisonous insects one by one with a lighted candle, so I took down the net, folded it into several long folds and began to shake it crosswise in the chamber, when one of the cord wings came flying and hit me on the back of my hand with such force that a faint shriek of pain escaped from my throat. The third time I got into bed I found myself a little calmer, but sleep I could not. Ten-thirty was the hour on the clock. Reflection was not a happy one. Why had I come to such a wretched place at all? If a middle-school teacher should have to deal with such fellows, he must indeed be a pitiable object. I wondered why the supply of middle-school teachers did not come short. Nobody but an honest fellow of exceeding patience would take up the vocation as life work. Having no such great patience, I thought the profession would never do for me. The chain of thought brought me around to the case of Kiyo, who seemed so noble. It is true that the old woman had neither education nor social rank, but none the less was the possessor of a noble character. My heart had never turned to her in gratitude before, though I had received so many kindnesses from her, but now that I was alone at a place so far from where she was living, my heart began to melt in grateful remembrance toward the kind woman. She said she would like to eat the *sasa-ame* of Echigo. The trouble of going so far as Echigo to get the cake for her would be amply repaid, for she really deserved it. My Kiyo would commend me saying that I had an unselfish, honest, frank character, but I am not worthy of such high praise, she deserves it instead. She is so noble and loving. Oh that I could see her now!

My heart and mind had all been occupied with the thoughts of Kiyo, when all at once bang, bang, bang, just above my head, came the sound of drumming feet on the floor made by some thirty or forty boys in number. I feared that the floor might come down upon my head. The drumming was followed by a war cry proportionately loud. Thinking something serious had happened, I sprang out of my bed. Then, only then, it struck me that the boys had done it out of vengeance. No crime could be canceled before a man apologized, confessing what he had done was wrong. His conscience would tell him he had done wrong. A right-minded man would go to bed and repent there from the bottom of his heart and come to ask forgiveness. Even if he did not come and ask pardon, at least he should, out of repentance, go to bed and be sleeping quietly. These fellows seemed to think the dormitory a pen in which they could get about just as much as pigs. "Do away with your madman's pranks. You shall smart for it." Thus saying to myself, I got out of the room in my nightgown and ran upstairs clearing the staircase in three-and-a-half strides. But, strange to say, the noise caused by the stamping on the floor had suddenly ceased and no voice, or even footsteps, could be heard at all. How could I account for this sudden calm? Was it a calm before a storm? The lamps had already been put out. Nothing could be seen distinctly through the darkness, but something told me very plainly that the mischief-doers were hiding themselves somewhere. The long corridor running from east to west had no crevice in which even a little mouse could hide. The moon was sending her resplendent rays toward the extremity of the passageway, and made it as bright as broad daylight. I wondered if I was not in a labyrinth walking around and around. I have been a great dreamer ever since a child. I remember that I sometimes sprang out of bed, talked some incoherent words and was greatly laughed at. One evening, when I was some seventeen years old, I had a dream in which I picked up a diamond. I started up and reproachfully demanded of my elder brother who slept beside me what he had done with the precious stone I had just picked up. Crest fallen was I for a couple of days, for I became the laughing stock of the whole family. So perhaps I had been dreaming, yet I was so sure of the trick the boys had played upon me a moment ago that I sat in the middle of the veranda and began to think what I should do next, when what should I hear but "One, two, three, Hurrah!" a shout of some forty boys in a chorus marking time with the stamping of feet on the floor! It was not a dream.

Then, crying in such a voice as to beat theirs, "Be quiet, young rascals. Don't you know it is the dead of night?" I began to run along the passage toward the spot whence the shout proceeded. Dark was the corridor along which I ran, the moonlit spot at the extremity of the passage being the only guide, for which I made with all my might. I had not gone six or seven yards when something hard lying in the middle of the veranda caught me by the leg. Bang I fell, a cry of pain escaping from my lips. With an oath, I sprang to my feet, but run I could not, for my legs would not obey the command of the brain, however impatient it was. Irritability drove me to run on with one leg, but what was my disappointment when reaching the spot, I heard neither the stamping of feet nor the sound of a human voice! Stillness reigned. However degenerate man might be, this seemed to me an extreme case utterly beyond my comprehension. They were no better than swine. Being pigs, they would never come out and apologize to me of their own accord. But they should know I would not concede even one single step until I should succeed in driving them out of their hiding places and punishing them one by one. Thus making up my mind, I tried to open one of the bed chambers in order to look inside, but the door would not open to my pulling or pushing. I tried ever so hard, yet either it was locked up or barred with desks or some such things, it was so very tight as if it were locked by magic. Then I tried the north chamber just opposite, but all to no avail. I was so eager and excited to open the door in order to catch the fellows inside that I was completely taken aback when I heard a war shout with a stamping of feet coming from the east end of the corridor. I knew at once that the boys were, by a previous arrangement, trying to attack me from both sides of the veranda, some from the east, others from the west, but I did not know what to do in such a fix.

To confess frankly, I have a fair share of courage but sadly lack tact, and was completely at a loss how to manage things as they presented themselves. However, it would never do for me to be beaten. My honor would be trodden down in the dust, if I should let things go on as they stood. An inexcusable shame would it be for a Yedo man to be called a coward. It would be an ineffaceable disgrace for me if I was teased by some dozen dirty-nosed urchins when on night duty, and not knowing what to do with them was compelled to smooth the matter down and let it go in silence. My ancestors were bodyguards to the Shogun; they all belonged to a very ancient stock of the Minamoto, a direct line of the Emperor Seiwa, that is to say, I am a descendent of the proud knight, Tada Mitsunaka. I am of noble birth—incomparably higher than those poor lowly peasant lads. The only drawback is that I lack tact; the only difficulty lies in the fact I am at a loss what to do in such cases. But never would I be beaten however hard pressed I might be. It is all the fault of my being honest. Yet if honesty could not be the final victor, what else could, I wonder? A moment's reflection will make it all plain. In case tonight will not bring me victory, tomorrow will. If that will not, the day after tomorrow surely will. In case the day after tomorrow should fail to bring me victory, I will order lunch from my boardinghouse and remain right there until my perseverance has been crowned with a glorious triumph. Thus making up my mind, I sat down in the middle of the long hall, and crossing my legs I waited bravely till dawn. Mosquitoes came buzzing, but their bites could not disturb me a bit. Feeling the part of shin hit by the hard block a few moments ago, my hand came upon something slippery. Probably it was bleeding. Let blood come out as much as it pleased. In the meanwhile, sleep had been busy working over my fatigued nature, and I fell fast asleep. Stir and commotion nearby awoke me from my slumber, and I jumped up with an oath. The door on the right of where I sat was half open and I found before me two of the boys standing and staring at me. As soon as I had recovered my senses and come to consciousness, taking hold of the nearest boy by the leg, I pulled him with all my might. Down he fell on his back with a great thud. "Served you right," I exclaimed. Scared by this act of mine, the other boy hesitated a moment before he took to his heels. I sprang after him like a wild beast and gave him two or three good shakes by the shoulder. The boy winked his eyes in an utter bewilderment. On my commanding them to follow me to my room, they came after me as meekly and submissively as sheep. The night had already dawned.

Cross-examination in my chamber, however, brought no satisfactory result. It failed to draw out any candid confessions from the boys. "Pigs are pigs." These fellows being no better than swine seemed to make, "We do not know," their first and last argument. In the meantime, the small room where the interrogation was going on became pretty full of visitors from the upstairs rooms, who had slipped in one after another. Every one of them had swollen sleepy eyes. Miserable wretches! One sleepless night, and they looked just as thin as ghosts. Man should be made of sterner stuff! I told them to go, wash their faces and come back to argue, yet nobody stirred.

Nearly an hour had been spent in endless questions and answers, when the Principal Badger made his sudden appearance. I learned afterward that the janitor had gone all the way to his house to report there was a disturbance in the school. He should never have been so alarmed as to call on the principal about such a trivial event. No better position than that of a middle-school janitor could have been obtained by such an alarmist, thought I. The principal heard through all I had to say. He too gave an ear to what the boys said. Then he told them to attend school as usual until they were given further notice. He dismissed the boys one and all with the words, "Wash your faces and have your breakfast right away, lest you should be late for school. Quick, boys!" What an example of indecision! Had I been in his place,

I would have turned out all the boarders right on the spot. Naturally such a lenient, lukewarm attitude of the principal would encourage the boys to slight the teachers on night duty. Turning to me then, the principal said that I must be very tired after so much anxiety, and that I should be excused for that day. "No," said I to him, "I had not the least anxiety. If such an event took place every night, I should never be troubled. Teaching I will do. One sleepless night, and were I unable to do my teaching I would return part of my salary to school." At this, the bewildered principal stared me in the face for some time and then told me that my face was much swollen. Indeed, I felt it somewhat heavy and dull. Moreover, it was so itchy all over. A hundred mosquitoes must have bitten it. Scratching it with both hands, I told him that, however swollen my face might be, it should never interfere with my teaching as long as my organ of speech was in good condition. "You are so full of energy," was his commendatory remark. I wonder, however, whether it was really a commendation. I dare say it was a bit of irony lanced at me.

Chapter 5

"Won't you go fishing with us?" said Red-shirt to me one day. Red-shirt is the possessor of such a sweet tongue as to give the hearer uneasiness. No one can tell him from a female by the mere ring of his voice. If a man, he should have a manly voice. Is not he a graduate of the Imperial University? I, a mere graduate of the Physics School, have a much bolder voice. It is a shame for a *bungakushi* to have such an effeminate voice!

"Well, —" I answered, as the invitation had little attraction for me. "Have you never been an angler?" was his next impolite question. "Yes, but not often." said I. "When a boy, I had the pleasure of catching three *funa* (a fish of the carp family) in the fishing pond at Komme. Again, on the fete day of Bishamon, Kagurazaka, I managed to hook a carp about eight inches long at the miniature pond and was about to cry out with rapture that I had caught a big fish, when down it fell into its own element with a splash. I still remember it with great regret." Upon this remark of mine, Red-shirt sticking out his long chin laughed with his usual ho! ho! I thought there was no special need of laughing in such an affected tone. "If that is the case, you do not yet know how much an angler enjoys his sport," he said. "I shall be only too glad to show you how to fish, if you desire." He was in high spirits. Never would I be shown how to fish by such a man.

You may be quite sure that those who are fond of fishing or hunting are all cruel, stony hearted. A merciful man will never find pleasure in killing living things. A fish or a bird will find it much pleasanter to live than to be put to death. In the case of one who has to earn his daily bread by fishing or hunting, it is another matter; but one who lives in luxury and says he can enjoy no sleep unless he kills some game is a perfect savage. This was the prevailing line of thought in my mind, yet he, being a *bungakushi,* was cleverer in speech, and thinking I should make him a poor match in argument, I kept silent. Upon this, Red-shirt thought he had the best of it and urged me to go with him that day if I had time. As to how to fish he would be very glad to show me. He continued that Mr. Yoshikawa's company without mine would be rather lonesome. His way of urging was so very persuasive. Mr. Yoshikawa was teacher of drawing with the nickname of Clown, you remember. This man for some secret reason called on Red-shirt day and night, and would follow him wherever Red-shirt went. Nobody would take him to be a colleague, but a servant. It was therefore no surprise to me when I heard that Clown was going with Red-shirt, for the former always kept company whenever the latter went out. One thing that puzzled me most was why he had invited such a blunt unsociable man as I to join them when they could go alone. I dare say the proud dean wanted to show me what a perfect angler he was by catching some big fish. Never should I be scared by such a shallow scheme. Two or three tunnies caught by Red-shirt would not make me stare in speechless amazement. Humble as I am, I am a man. Though a poor fisherman, I could catch something if I let down my line. If I should not go now, the suspicious dean would think that I did not go because

I was a poor hand at fishing, and not because I disliked the sport. Under the circumstances just mentioned, I could not but answer, "Yes, I will go."

After school, I went home, got ready, went to the station and waited a good while, before Red-shirt and Clown made their appearance. We three went down to the beach together. Only one boatman was to manage a long narrow boat, the shape of which was quite new to us born in Tokyo. I had been looking around the boat, but had noticed no rod. Thinking nobody could fish without a rod, I asked the artist how it was. "In fishing far out in the open sea, you need no rod, but a line," he calmly answered, stroking his chin. He looked as if he were a professional angler. Silence would have saved me from disgrace. I was very sorry I had asked the question of Noda, the Clown.

Slow was the rowing of the boatman, yet experience is a great thing, and on looking back, we found we were far out, the beach looking so very small in the distance. The top of the pagoda of the temple called Kohakuji was seen tapering into a pin from the midst of the woods. In front, we saw the Green Island floating on the surface of the sea. This is an uninhabited island, where only rocks and pines are found. Nobody can live in a place with nothing but rocks and pines. Red-shirt was looking at the beautiful scenery and admiring it. Noda, the Clown, was saying it was an unsurpassed view. I did not know whether it was a matchless scene or not, but certainly it gave me a pleasurable feeling. I thought it would do me good to breathe in the salt breeze on the broad, boundless sea. I felt very hungry.

"Look at that pine tree. Its trunk is so straight and it spreads upward like an open umbrella. Turner would have drawn such a tree," Red-shirt was saying to Noda, the Clown. "Yes, it is a genuine Turner. What a perfect curve! A Turner itself!" was the self-satisfied response of Noda. I did not know what they meant by Turner. But thinking the ignorance would give me no inconvenience, I kept silent.

The boat turned around the isle on the right. No waves, no ripples. Nobody would think it a sea. It was so perfectly smooth. True the pleasure I enjoyed was due to the kindness of Red-shirt. Thinking it would be fine to get on the island, I inquired if the boat could not be steered for the place where a big rock stood. "Well, it could, but it would never do for fishing to go too near the shore," Red-shirt objected, and I shut my mouth. Then Noda officiously proposed this, "What do you think, my dear dean, of calling that island 'Turner Isle' hereafter?" "Well, it is a good idea. Yes, we shall call the island by that name," agreed the dean. If in that 'we' I were included, I would object to it. "Green Isle" was good enough for me. "What would you say, my dear dean, if we placed Madonna by Raphael on that rock? Don't you think it would make a fine picture?" Noda said to Red-shirt. "Let us not dwell upon that subject any longer," he answered with his usual, disagreeable ho! ho! ho! "You need not worry about that; it is perfectly safe, for there is nobody here to interfere." With this, Noda turned around and gave me a glance. Withdrawing his eyes at once, he smiled up his sleeves.

This maneuver of theirs gave me an indefinably disagreeable feeling. I did not care a pin whether it was Madonna or *kodanna* (young master). They could place her or him anywhere they pleased. But saying things unintelligible to others and not caring whether others understand, is mean, base, ignoble conduct on the part of anybody. The behavior of Noda, the Clown, was exactly that, and still he proudly called himself a Yedo man. Madonna, thought I, must be the secret name of the dancing girl with whom the dean was in love, or some such thing. Placing his favorite *geisha* under a pine tree on an uninhabited island, Red-shirt stares at her admiringly at a short distance in order to give the picture a good effect. This would be quite ideal to him, and if Noda, the artist, represented the scene in an oil painting and exhibited it at an art gallery, it would be the climax of Red-shirt's happiness.

Saying the place was a good one, the boatman stopped rowing and cast anchor. "How deep?" asked Red-shirt. "About six fathoms," was the answer. "It is not deep enough to find *tai*." With this, he cast his line into the water. He seemed to think that he could pull up such a big fish. Too ambitious, I should think. "Certainly my dean's skill will entice a *tai*, and the sea is perfectly calm." Thus dropping a complimentary remark, Noda, the Clown, also letting out his line, cast it to the bottom. It had nothing but a bit of lead at the end. It served as the weight, but it had no float. If one could fish without a cork, one would be able to know one's fever without the help of a thermometer as well.

Thinking it no use to try, I was just watching what they were doing, when Red-shirt said to me, "Well, won't you try, have you no line?" "Yes, I have a line long enough, but no float," I answered. "A novice needs a float. We need no float." Thus saying, he tried to show me how it was done. "When the baited end of the line has reached the bottom," he continued, "you just put the part of the line you hold on the side of the boat, and manage it with your forefinger. If there is a bite, you'll feel it right away." "Well, I have one," he said, and began to haul in his line hand over hand. There was no fish and the bait was gone. It served him right. "My dear dean, I'm very sorry for you. It must have been a big fish," said Noda, the flatterer. "If your skill could not secure it, nobody could, today; yet you are far superior, although you have missed the fish, compared to him who stares at the cork all day long. He is like one who cannot ride on a bicycle without a brake."

These ironical, sarcastic remarks of Noda irritated me not a little, and I wanted more than once to deal him good sound blows with my fist. "I am a man as well as they. Red-shirt, the dean, can never monopolize such a broad sea, though he may pretend to have rented it. At least a bonito or two would give me a bite for sheer love." Thus thinking, I dropped my line with the plummet and waited for a bite, letting go and hauling it in a little with my finger tips. In a few moments, something gave a big pull at the end of the line. "This must be a fish. An inanimate thing can never give such a strong pull. Good Heavens! Yes, I have it." Thus thinking, I began to haul in the line quickly. "Well, have you caught something? You are quite promising!" came a sarcastic remark from Noda. In the meanwhile, the line had almost been hauled in, and only five feet or so remained in the water. Looking into the water from the side of the boat, I saw a striped fish like a gold fish in shape, which struggling right and left, came up to the surface as I tugged the line. "Splendid!" I cried. As the fish came out of the water, it gave a great splash, and I had my face washed with salt water. I had no little difficulty in boating it, but still harder was it to take off the hook. My hand got disagreeably greasy. Vexation made me throw it with all my might in the middle board of the boat. It moved no longer. Red-shirt and Noda were amazed to see this act of mine. Vigorously washing my hands in the water, I brought them to my nose, and found they still had a disagreeable smell. One trial was quite enough. I would never again take hold of any fish I caught, however big it might be; neither would the fish want to be seized by me. No time was lost in winding and putting away the line.

"The first battle won is a meritorious exploit, but a *goruki*—," remarked the assuming Noda again. Upon this, Red-shirt observed that the name of *goruki* sounded like that of a Russian man of letters (he meant Gorki). This was how he tried a play upon words. "Yes, exactly, my dear dean," agreed Noda, the Clown. There is no doubt Gorki is a Russian literary man; Maruki is a photographer in Shiba; and the rice-bearing plant *(ki)* is a sustainer of human life. A very bad habit had this Redshirt, who always gave the names of foreigners in square characters *(katakana)* whenever he came across a man. Everyone has his own speciality. A teacher of mathematics like myself can never tell a Gorki from a *shariki* (a coolie). He ought to be a little more considerate. The "Autobiography of Benjamin Franklin," or "Pushing to the Front," is not unknown even to me. He had better mention these names. I often noticed that he brought to school a red-covered magazine called *Teikoku Bungaku* (Imperial literature) and was reverentially reading it. On asking, I was told by Porcupine that all the names of square characters given by Red-shirt came from that periodical. If so, *Teikoku Bungaku* is quite a bad, misleading magazine, I should think.

In the meantime, Red-shirt and Noda had eagerly been fishing, and in an hour or so, they had caught about a dozen fish. Funny to say, every one of them was a *goruki*. No *tai* was polite enough to be caught by them. "Russian literature seems to be very popular today," Red-shirt was saying to Noda. "Well, if your skill fails to catch anything but *goruki,* no wonder I have caught nothing else," Noda was answering. The boatman told me that the small fish is full of bones, and is not good to eat; that it is fit for only fertilizer. Both the dean and the poor artist were, so to speak, fishing for fertilizer. I even felt sorry for them. One of the fertilizer fish was quite enough for me. Throwing myself on my back in the middle of the boat, I looked up at the beautiful sky. This, thought I, was far nicer and more elegant than catching *goruki*.

Then the two began to talk in a whisper. I could not distinctly hear what they were saying, nor did I care. On my part,

I was looking up into the blue firmament and thinking about Kiyo, my old nurse. Had I money and could bring her down to such a beautiful place, what a pleasure and delight it would give her! The matchless scenery would cry out against such a companion as Noda, the flatterer. Kiyo is an old woman with a wrinkled face, but nobody would be ashamed of her wherever he took her. Such a mean fellow as Noda would be unbearable either in a carriage, on board a ship, or on the top of Ryounkaku Tower, Asakusa. Were I the dean, and Red-shirt I, Noda would certainly say nice things to me and throw sarcasm at Red-shirt. People say that a Yedo man is insincere, and I can hardly contradict this saying when such a rascal as Noda goes about in the country places, making out repeatedly that he is a genuine Yedo man. The people in the country would naturally come to the conclusion that insincerity is another name for a Yedo man and a Yedo man is insincerity itself.

My mind had been occupied with some such thoughts, when the two began to laugh in a suppressed manner. I listened, but could hardly make out what they were talking about, for interruptions occurred so often in their conversation. "Well? I doubt it." "It is perfectly true, but he does not know. It is quite a pity!" "You don't say so." "A grasshopper — it is true."

Little attention had I been paying to other words, but when the word "grasshopper" slipped off from Noda's lips, I at once came to attention. Strange to say, Noda put an especial emphasis upon the word "grasshopper" and made it very distinctly plain to me, while all other words lost their meanings. "Again, that Hotta." "Well, yes, it may be so." "*Tempura*, ha! ha! ha!" "Setting him up." "Dumpling, too."

Frequent interruptions made it hardly possible for me to follow, yet judging from the words "grasshopper," "*tempura*," and "dumpling," etc., I was quite sure that the subject of their confidential talk was myself. Conversation should be carried on in loud voices; and if they wanted to have a private talk, they should never have invited me to join. Damned be these fellows! Were it a *batta* (grasshopper), or a *setta* (a kind of sandal), the fault did not lie in me. As Principal Badger requested me to permit him to take the whole matter into his hands, I simply acquiesced for the time being out of respect to his position; and Noda, the Clown, should never have meddled with it; he had better sit still in the corner sucking his paint brush. I would sooner or later attend to my own business and bring it to a satisfactory solution. But that was not the thing that gave me uneasiness. What troubled me most lay in such words as "That Hotta," "Instigation, etc." Did he mean that Hotta had set me up, and made the agitation bigger, or Hotta had instigated the boys to persecute me? I was quite at a loss how to make it out.

Looking up into the sky, I noticed that the sun was going down and a cool breeze had sprung up. A thin cloud like the smoke rising from an incense stick was seen spreading over the transparent bosom of the firmament, and, losing itself in the depth, again appeared in the form of a light fog.

"Let us go home," said Red-shirt all at once, as if the thought had come as revelation. "Yes, it is quite time to be going," answered Noda, the flatterer. "Do you expect to see your Madonna tonight?" "Don't speak nonsense, man, for it may lead to some mistake," reproved Red-shirt, as he raised himself a little from his reclining posture against the boat side. "Ha! Ha! It's perfectly safe!" returned Noda. "If he did hear . . . ." Upon his turning toward me, I cast an angry glance from my big wide opened eyes right upon the face of Noda, who, dazzled by the sudden shoot of light from my eyes, withdrew his eyes saying, "I cannot stand it." Shrugging his shoulders, he scratched his head. What a sniveling, whining scoundrel!

The boat was slowly making for the shore. "You don't seem to like fishing," remarked Red-shirt. "Well, no. It is far better and nicer to lie and look up into the sky," I answered, and threw into the water the stump of the cigarette I had been enjoying, which with a hissing sound floated off at the mercy of the waves along the wake made by the strokes of the oars.

"Your coming to the school is welcomed by the students, and I hope you will please do your best." These words of the dean had nothing to do with fishing. They were an entirely out-of-place remark. "I am not so welcome to them, I know," I answered. "Yes, you are. It is not a mere compliment. They are really glad, are they not, Mr. Yoshikawa?" "Well, they are more than glad; they are greatly excited over your advent," Noda answered with an ironical smile. Strange to say, every word uttered by him called forth indignation in my mind. "Yet you will not be safe if you do not take care," added Red-shirt. "Well, I am already aware of the danger and am quite ready to face it," I replied. The alternative was either to resign or to bring all the boarders down to their knees to apologize to me. "Don't express yourself so positively, or I shall be at a loss what to do," pleaded the dean. "Indeed the warning I gave to you came from the dis-interested good will I entertain toward you and it would be pretty hard for me if you took it amiss." "Our dean is truly a well-wisher of yours. Both coming from Yedo, we should help each other, and though of little influence, I am privately doing my best in order to have you stay in the school as long as you possibly can." These were the only words of ordinary human kindness ever uttered by Noda, the Clown. I would sooner hang myself than to be under obligation to him.

"Yet the boys are all very glad to have you come. However, the circumstances are so very complicated that simple honesty alone can hardly penetrate. There may have arisen, and may arise, an event or two to arouse your anger, but believing that patience is the prescribed dose, please keep cool and quiet as I am doing, and I will do my best to promote your interests, you know."

"Various complicated circumstances? What are they?" "They are too crooked and entangled. They will be clear and plain to you by-and-by. Time will be sure to disclose all without my explaining them now, won't it, Mr. Yoshikawa?"

"Yes, they are very complicated as the dean says. A day or two will not give any satisfactory solution, but the circumstances will gradually come to light, and I am sure that time will make our telling them entirely unnecessary." Noda repeated in the very words of Red-shirt.

"If they are so very complicated and troublesome, I had better not have an explanation. I would never have asked you to explain if you had not first introduced the subject."

"It is very true," answered Red-shirt. "Mere introduction of the subject will not do unless the important point be disclosed. I will then tell you this much. It may be impolite, but you are just fresh from college, and have had no experience as a teacher. Contrary to your expectations, school is, so to speak, a storehouse of complicated circumstances, where one's straightforwardness will hardly do."

"If simple honesty will not do, what will, I wonder?"

"Well, that you are so unsophisticated shows your want of experience."

"It goes without saying that I lack experience; it is very plainly and distinctly written out in the record of my personal history. I am but twenty-three years and four months old."

"That is the very point, where an unexpected danger will present itself from unexpected quarters."

"As long as I am honest, I shall be afraid of nobody who may take advantage of me."

"Of course, you need fear nobody, but you will be imposed upon. It actually happened that your predecessor had a bitter experience. That is why I warn you so earnestly."

Wondering why the talkative Noda kept so still and quiet, I looked back and saw him eagerly engaged in conversation on fishing with the boatman in the back part of the boat. We two could talk far better by ourselves. "Who do you say took advantage of my predecessor?" I resumed.

"It would hardly be fair for me to give the name of the man, or his honor would be entirely ruined, and having no definite evidence against him, I shall be blamed if I do. Anyway, now that you are here, I hope you will succeed, and we should be very much disappointed if you did otherwise. Please be more careful," said Red-shirt.

"It is easily said, but hard to act upon," I answered. "It would be all right, provided I did no wrong, would it not?"

He laughed at this remark of mine with his usual ho! ho! I was quite sure that I had said nothing laughable. I was firmly convinced till now that this principle of simple honesty would hold good for all time. The majority of people seem to encourage each other to grow bad. They seem to believe that success in the world will come only to those who are bad, or have become bad. When they meet with a rare specimen of pure simplicity, they contemptuously criticize and call him "A boy-master, or a greenhorn." How is it then that the teacher of ethics, both in a primary school and an academy, teaches his boys to be honest and never to tell a lie? He had better not, but rather teach them boldly how to tell a lie, how to impose upon a man, or to suspect others. This would be far better and more profitable both to the world at large, and to the person who learns it.

Red-shirt's "ho! ho!" certainly meant that my frankness was not to his taste. There would be no help for me but to be laughed at, if simplicity and frankness could not get along in the world. My Kiyo never laughed at such a time, but so sympathetically did she listen to me that Red-shirt looked far inferior to her in my estimation.

"To be doing right is, of course, good as you say, but that alone will never save you from the snares people set for you, if you fail to know how bad they are. You must know there are persons who look very cheerful and open hearted, who will so kindly see to your board and lodging, and yet you will have to be watchful. Autumn seems to be setting in with its coolness. A fog like sepia has spread itself over the beach. A wonderful view! What do you say, my dear Mr. Yoshikawa? Don't you think it's just admirable? Behold! that view over the shore." Thus Red-shirt addressed Noda, the Clown, in a loud voice.

"Yes, it is just wonderful! I would put it into my folio if I had time. I am very sorry to leave it behind." Thus agreeing with Red-shirt, he gave a big beat upon his professional drum (stomach). (A Japanese clown's musical instrument is a drum.)

A light was seen upstairs in Minatoya, the hotel. A whistle from a locomotive was heard through the still air of evening when the boat we were in, reaching the shore, thrust its bow onto the beach. The landlady of the hotel, standing on the beach, gave the dean a polite salutation with the words, "Good evening, sir, welcome home." As for me, I jumped down with a yell from the boat upon the sands.

Chapter 6

I dislike Noda, the flatterer. Japan will gain much if such a fellow be sent down to the bottom of the sea with a millstone around his neck. I have an aversion to Red-shirt because of his voice. I can assure you that his natural voice is rough, but from affectation he is trying hard to show people how sweet his voice is. He may put on airs as much as he wishes, but his features will gain little favor with the fair sex save Madonna, or some such coquette. But being dean, he speaks far harder things than the poor artist. On the way home, I considered what he had told me, and thought there were some reasons for his warning. True he had never given me any definite facts, by which I could conjecture who the devil was, yet his admonition seemed to be directed against the person of Porcupine himself. If so, why could he not say so plainly? It was not a manly way. And were Porcupine such a rascal, he had better dismiss him at once. Even a *bungakushi* turns out to be a mere puppet when placed in the post of dean. He who cannot openly give out the name of the wrong-doer in a confidential talk must be a weakling. A weakling is generally kindly disposed, and Red-shirt seems to have womanly kindness. Kindness is one thing; voice is another. To dislike one's voice is not to blot out one's kindness. It would be a misdirected action. Be that as it may, a mystery is the world, where he to whom one has an instinctive aversion is kind, while those to whom one can open his heart as friends are rascals. They must be making a fool of me here. In all probabilities, as this is an out-of-the-way country place, topsy-turvydom seems to be a prevailing feature contrary to Tokyo. Peace does not seem to dwell here. It is a dangerous place. Before long, I may see fire become ice; *tofu* stone. But nobody could believe that Porcupine would incite his students; mischief does not seem to exist in his nature. True he could do almost anything if he would, as he was said to be the most popular teacher among the boys. However, he need not take such a roundabout method; he could directly come and pick a quarrel with me, and it would save him a great deal of trouble. If I were in the way, he could ask me to resign, giving me the reasons why I was an obstacle. Thus a great deal of time and trouble would be saved. A talk together would bring us into a better understanding. I should not hesitate to give up my position as soon as tomorrow, provided the reasons he gave were just and sincere. Bread might be had not only here in this place, but anywhere I might go. Wherever I might roam about I was sure I should not be so wretched as to lead the life of a dog. I thought Porcupine a more sensible fellow.

It was Porcupine himself who treated me with ice water, when I first came here. To be treated even with a single cup of ice water by such a double-faced scoundrel would be a contamination upon my character. He had to pay only one-and-a-half sen as I took only one glass, yet whether it was a single sen or a half sen I would never be a debtor to a swindler, or else I should feel bad until the day of my death. "He shall have one-and-a-half sen tomorrow when I go to school. I have a loan of three yen from Kiyo, which I have not yet returned, although five years have passed. Do not think I cannot pay it back, but I will not, for the noble Kiyo will never dream of being paid back;

she never lends me money in prospect of my greater income. On my part too, it would be a sin to think of returning it, as it would indicate that the tie binding us is based on duty and not upon affection. The more I think of such a thing, the greater pain would it give Kiyo, for it might mean that I doubted the purity of her mind. It is true the debt has not been paid back, but it is not because I considered it nothing, but because I think her a part of my own flesh and blood. Although comparison of Porcupine with the noble Kiyo would be absurd, yet I owe a debt of gratitude to him by whom I was treated, were it cheap ice water, or sweet tea. I do not express it with my lips, because I regard him as a true man and deem silence an act of good will toward him. If I pay my share, it will cancel all, but to keep it in my heart as a sacred debt will be a far greater return present than gold can buy. True I am a man of neither rank nor title, but simply a plain, independent man. If an independent man bows down his head, it would be a more precious gift than one million yen.

"The one-and-a-half sen Porcupine paid for me has been a means of his procuring a reward from me more precious than one million yen. He should esteem it an obligation to me; yet to secretly hatch up a scheme against me! Base, ignoble rascal! So soon as I pay him that cursed fraction of money tomorrow, I shall be neither creditor nor debtor. Then the field will be open to take issue with him."

I thought thus far, when sleep, which had been busy trying to make me her prey succeeded, and I fell fast asleep. The next day, having a plan known only to me, I went to school much earlier than usual and waited for Porcupine to come. He was very slow to make his appearance that morning. First came Green Squash. Then the teacher of Chinese Classics; then Noda, the Clown. Lastly Red-shirt made his grand appearance, but Porcupine's desk was so innocently quiet with a piece of chalk laid lengthwise on it as if it were waiting for its owner to come. Intending to give it back to Porcupine as soon as I went into the teachers' room, I had carried all the way from home one-and-a-half sen in my palm, as is done in going to the public bath. Mine being a greasy hand, I found on opening that the money was wet with sweat. Thinking he would object to accepting the wet money, I placed the coppers on the desk, blew them two or three times and put them back into my palm again, when Red-shirt came and apologized to me, saying he had given me much trouble the previous day. "No, indeed." said I, "Thanks to your kindness, I got as hungry as a wolf." At this, the dean resting his elbow on the desk of Porcupine brought his even flat face so near my nose that I wondered what he was going to do. No sooner had he finished this maneuver than he said to me, "Please keep between you and me the talk we had yesterday on our return. I hope it has been disclosed to no-body yet." Being the possessor of a feminine voice, Red-shirt seemed to be an overanxious soul. Certainly I had yet told it to nobody, but to be bound by an oath not to disclose it was an awful handicap to me, since I had carried the coppers all the time in my palm intending a disclosure. The dean should have been a little bolder. True he had never said the schemer was Porcupine, yet enough had been said to enable one to guess who it was. Now he wanted me not to solve the riddle as it was inconvenient to him. It was an act of injustice inexcusable for a dean. Properly he ought to have come forth into the heat of the fight Porcupine and I were engaged in, publicly taken my side and stood by me till the last. Then he would deservedly be called a good head teacher, and the honorable title "Red-shirt" given him would be justified.

"Well, nobody has heard it yet, but I am going to open a ne-gotiation with Porcupine," I answered. Upon this, great consternation taking hold of him made him say, "Do not do such a thing, or great trouble will ensue. I do not remember that I have ever criticized Mr. Hotta in your presence. I shall be placed in a fix if you act so rashly. You have not come to this school to stir up a disturbance?" At this strange remark, which made no sense, I told him it would hardly be fair on my part to draw salary and brew trouble from which the school would greatly suffer. "Then never divulge what we talked about yesterday; just keep it merely as a reference," asked Red-shirt piteously with perspiration on his forehead. "Well, I shall also be annoyed, but if it gives you so much trouble, I shall be silent about it," I assured him. "Are you quite sure?" he asked me again, probably for the sake of assurance. Nobody could fathom how far down his effeminacy lay. I thought a *bungakushi* much more manly. If he were made of such poor stuff, I know of nobody who would like to be one. Red-shirt was not a bit ashamed to be inconsistent and illogical in his demands. Moreover, he was impertinent enough as to doubt my integrity. Begging your pardon, I expect I am a man through and through. Come, search into the nook and corner of my heart to find even a mote of baseness which makes me betray others, slighting the promise I have solemnly made, and you will only reap disappointment.

By this time, the desk on each side of me had been occupied by its owner, and the dean hastily returned to his own seat. He has an affected manner of walking. Walking up and down the room, he noiselessly lets down the soles of his shoes. I did not know till then that a noiseless gait is a virtue to be proud of. Do not imitate that unless you are going to be a thief. Try to be an ordinary man with an ordinary step. In the meantime, the bugle was sounded inviting both teachers and boys to begin their work. Porcupine failed to appear before school began, and I had to leave the money on his desk and hasten to the classroom.

The lesson of the first period had kept me a little longer in class and on coming back to the teachers' room, I found the teachers had all returned and were having a chat at their desks, Porcupine among them. I thought he had stayed away from school that day, but he was only a little late. No sooner had he seen me than he said he had been behind time on account of me and demanded a fine of me. I took up the coppers from the desk, laid them before him and said the money was the price of ice I had taken the other day on the main street. I asked him to take and put them back into his pocket. He was going to make fun of me, calling it nonsense, but seeing me rather serious, he swept the money back to my desk, telling me it was a stupid joke. Willy-nilly, was I destined to be treated by him after all?

"It's not a joke; I am in earnest," I said. "I have no reason to be treated with ice water by you and I mean to pay; you have no good reason to refuse."

"If you are so scrupulous about the cursed one-and-a-half sen, I shall not be so obstinate as to refuse," he answered. "But will you please explain why you did not pay sooner, but have waited till now, as if the thought came like a lightning flash?" "It matters little whether it is right now, or some other time," I replied "I do not like to have you stand the treat; I want to pay, that is all." Porcupine, who had coolly been staring me in the face, said "Pooh!" At this, I would have exposed his baseness and fought him but for Red-shirt's request, yet I could not make even a move since I had promised to be silent about it. He should never have said "Pooh!" when the other became so red-hot in anger.

"Yes, I shall take the price of ice water," he said, "but get out of the house where you board."

"Take the money and I am content," I returned. "I am perfectly free to leave the boardinghouse or to stay there right on."

"No," he said, "that will not do. The master of the house you board with called upon me yesterday and asked me to tell you to leave the room you are in. I demanded the reasons, which he gave. I thought them quite reasonable, but considering it very important to inquire more carefully, I called at his house this morning and heard the particulars."

What he had been talking about gave me no meaning. "How am I to know what the master told you?" I said. "Is it just for you to be so self-satisfied? Is it not proper for you to let me know the reasons if you have any? You have told me from the start that the master is in the right, and I am in the wrong. I tell you it is impertinence itself."

"Well, then you shall know," returned he. "Your rudeness has made you unbearable in that boardinghouse. A hostess differs from a servant-girl. It is a little too haughty an act to stretch out your feet and tell her to wipe them clean."

"When did I make her wipe my feet?" I demanded.

"I am not so sure of it," he replied, "but it is a fact that they are at a loss what to do with you. You are a nuisance to them. The ten or fifteen yen they get from you for board and lodging a month could easily be earned, the host said, by selling one hanging picture."

"Braggart! swindler! why did he then invite me to make my home with them, I wonder?"

"I do not know why. They asked you to come and live with them, that is true; but now they want you no more and wish you would leave them immediately. Do leave!"

"Of course, I will. I will not stay there a moment longer, if they should clasp their hands in supplication. You are to blame to have taken me to the home of such an impostor."

"I am to blame, or you are in the wrong. It is one or the other."

Quick tempered as I am, Porcupine is no less so; and we were quarreling in as loud voices as we possibly could make, each striving to beat the other in loudness. All the people in the room were looking at us, wondering what the matter was. They looked quite foolish with their chins hung down. Having done nothing unworthy of me as far as I remembered, I stood up in the middle of the room and gave each one a deliberate stare. All were scared by it, save Noda, the Clown, who smiled a complacent smile. When, however, my big, sharp penetrating eyes rested upon his gourdlike face, as if asking if he was ready to pick a quarrel with me, he all at once became very serious and polite. Terror, I presume, had come upon him. In the meanwhile, the bugle was sounded, and we, laying the quarrel on the table, both carried our steps toward the classrooms.

In the afternoon, there was a teachers' meeting to discuss how to deal with the boys who had acted rudely toward me the other night. Meetings being a new experience, I did not know what it would be. I thought it was something in which each of the teachers would express himself as he pleased and the principal would form out of the different opinions a decision according to his convenience. However, the term decision is generally used in the case where you can hardly tell good from bad. The card under consideration was of so plain a nature that no sane man would object to the punishing of the ill-behaved boys, and therefore it was a time-wasting meeting. Look at it from every viewpoint, and no different opinion would be brought forth. The case was too plain to necessitate the call of a teachers' meeting. It was quite proper for the principal himself to attend to and manage it at his own discretion. The meeting was ample proof of his lack of decision. Were such the general character of a principal, indecision and principal would go together as synonyms.

The meeting was held in the long narrow room next to the principal's; ordinarily it served as the dining room. About twenty black-leather cushioned chairs were arranged around a table. It looked altogether like a restaurant room in Kanda. The chair at the end of the table was occupied by the principal; next to him sat Red-shirt, the dean. We were then free to take any of the seats, but teachers of physical exercise were modest enough to take always the seats at the foot of the table. It being the first case with me, I wedged in my person between the teacher of history and the teacher of Chinese Classics. Opposite me sat Porcupine with Noda, the Clown, whose aspect was so mean and shabby however favorably one might look upon it. Enemy as he was, Porcupine had a much more picturesque face. I remember at the time of my father's funeral I saw a face much like his in the hanging picture on the hall of the Temple called Yogenji, Kobinata, Tokyo. On inquiry, the priest told me that the owner of the countenance was the monster named *Itaten*. Anger that day made his eyes big and round like an owl's, which he frequently focused at me. I was not to be intimidated in that way. Defeat was what I disliked most. Opening my eyes as wide as I possibly could, I stared him in the face. It is true the shape of my eyes is not so attractive, but as for their size, they beat everyone. "You will certainly make a great success as an actor, as you have such big eyes," Kiyo used to say.

At the request of the principal, who asked if all were present, Kawamura, the clerk, began to count one, two, three and said one was still missing. He thought and wondered who it was. It was nothing to be wondered at. Mr. Green Squash had not made his appearance yet. I do not know by what affinity we were bound, but I could never forget him since I first met him. I entered the teacher's room, and there the first object upon which my eyes rested was his meditative face. I was taking a walk, and there I saw his melancholy figure in my mind's eye. I went to the hot spring, and there I often saw his pale face in the bath tank. I gave him a greeting, and he made me the profoundest bow out of much deference. I had great compassion for him. Nobody in the school was so quiet and meek as he. He seldom smiled. He never spoke more than was needed. I find the word "sage" in books. I thought it was only found in a dictionary, but never in a person alive. I have, however, been convinced since I saw him that the word was well represented in Mr. Green Squash.

Having such intense interest in him, I at once noticed upon entering the conference room that he was not there. In fact, on attending the meeting, I expected to sit beside this good man, thinking he would surely be there. The principal said he expected him any moment, and unfolding the purple silk cloth parcel placed before him, he took out some mimeographed documents and began to read. As for Red-shirt, he commenced wiping his amber pipe with his silk handkerchief. This seemed to be his favorite pursuit, and I thought it was quite becoming to him. Each one of us was having a talk in a whisper with our neighbor, while those who had no companions were indulging in the art of scribbling on the table with the rubber ends of their pencils. Noda, the Clown, now and again addressed Porcupine, who, not so ready to join him, cast at him only some such ejaculation as "ugh," or "ah!" He repeatedly looked toward me and gave me a terrible glance. I was not to be beaten and gave back stares more terrible than his.

Long had we been waiting for Mr. Green Squash, who at last appeared and apologized to Principal Badger, saying he was very sorry to have kept us all waiting for him; that he had had business to attend to; and so forth. The meeting was then called to order; the mimeographed papers were then distributed among the teachers by clerk Kawamura. The first was how to punish the bad boys; the second, how to give them better discipline, with two or more items. Principal Badger then with as much dignity as usual stood up and made the following speech in such a grand manner as if he were an incarnation of education. He said, "Whenever a fault is committed or a wrong is done either by a teacher or a student, I always look upon it as a natural outcome of my lack of virtue. Whenever an unfortunate event happens, I am ashamed to know what an unworthy principal I am, who fails to fulfill his assigned duties. Unfortunately such an event has taken place this time, and I have the misfortune of apologizing to you all. However, what has happened has happened and there can be no help for it. The only way open to us now is to consider how to manage it satisfactorily. The particulars of the event are all known to you, so that I need not dwell upon them. I should be very much obliged to you if you would kindly and frankly speak out your minds for my reference as to the best method we should adopt on this occasion."

I heard him through, and thought what clever things a principal or a badger could speak. If the principal actually believed that he was alone responsible for the trouble and really thought it was his own fault, it would have been better for him to resign his post first instead of punishing the boys at all. Then such a nuisance as a meeting would have been unnecessary. Common sense would tell you that the fault lay neither in the principal nor in me, but entirely in the boys who behaved very rudely toward the teacher who was quietly performing his duty as night watch. Were Porcupine the actual instigator of the boys, he had better be punished with the boys. It would have settled the whole affair once and for all. Search throughout the world, and you will fail to find another who, taking all responsibilities upon himself, says he is responsible and is to blame for the act others are guilty of. This is a trick no other creature than a badger could perform. After delivering this illogical speech, the principal complacently looked all around him. Nobody dared to open his mouth. The teacher of natural history was looking at the crow perched on the roof of the first classroom; the teacher of Chinese Classics was folding and unfolding the printed paper; while Porcupine stared me in the face. If a meeting were such a foolish, meaningless thing, it would be far better for one to stay away and have a nap instead.

I got too impatient to sit still, and thinking to make an eloquent speech I was about to stand up, when Red-shirt was noticed just beginning to speak, and I stopped. He had, it seemed, put away his pipe and was saying something. He was seen wiping the perspiration on his face with his silk handkerchief, which, by-the-by, he must have confiscated from Madonna herself. I say a gentleman should use a snow-white linen handkerchief. He said, "I am sorry to hear of the unfortunate event caused by the rude boys in the dormitory. I am greatly ashamed as dean that my discipline of them was not thorough, and my influence upon them was not strong enough to prevent them from behaving rudely toward their teacher. Such a thing always happens whenever there is weakness somewhere. A superficial observer may think the fault lies entirely in the students, but if one goes a little deeper and inquires into the matter more carefully, one will perhaps find the responsibility all lies in the school itself. Therefore, it may not be a wise policy for the future to inflict severe punishment upon the boys by looking simply on the surface of the event. Moreover, being lads full of life and energy, they may be tempted to do naughty things. They may not have thought it bad, or rather may have done it half-unconsciously. Although the mode of punishment lies entirely in the hands of the principal himself, and I have no right to interfere with it, still I wish, if it could be wished, that he would be lenient and considerate enough to inflict upon them as light punishment as he possibly could." With this, Red-shirt resumed his seat much elated.

Badger is clever; Red-shirt is no less so. They both declared that the boys were not to blame when they were naughty, but the teacher. A man of mental derangement strikes you on the head. You are bad and the lunatic strikes you. Thus their logic goes on. Happy stars! If the boys are full of energy, let them go out into the playground and have wrestling. Unbearable it would be if grasshoppers were thrown into one's bed half-unconsciously. If this goes on and on, one's head will be cut off and carried away while one is asleep, and they will set the head-hunters free, saying it has partly been done out of unconsciousness.

Such was the line of thought along which my mind trudged. I had thought to say something, but if I spoke at all, it would never do unless I could do so eloquently as to make the hearers wonder stricken. Anger, however, makes me stammer in speech making, and usually chokes me to a full stop after I have uttered two or three words. It is my peculiar weakness. Badger and Red-shirt are far below me in character, but they are much cleverer in speech, and it would never do for me to be found fault with for a slip of the tongue. Let me mediate what I should say on the occasion, and I began to build up a fine speech in my mind, when I was surprised to see Noda, the Clown, suddenly stand up to speak. It was extremely assuming on the part of the poor artist to express his poor opinion. He spoke in his usual pert manner. "The grasshopper, and the war cry, affairs, which unfortunately happened this time are very deplorable events, which make us, well-wishers of the school, entertain doubts and fears about the future prosperity of the school. We teachers should, on this occasion, reflect on and examine our own conduct so as to help make the discipline of the school better. Therefore, that which both the principal and the dean have just said is good and to the point, and I have the honor of supporting it thoroughly. It is my earnest wish that lenient measures should be taken in dealing with the boys." What the artist said had many words, but very little sense. He profusely used classical Chinese words, but what I made out of his speech was only the sentence, "I support it with all my heart."

I hardly understood what Noda, the Clown, said, but, as it irritated me beyond control, I stood up before the outlines of my intended speech were fairly formed. "I disagree with him from head to foot," I began, but no other words coming to my succor, I added, "Well—I dislike such nonsense—such an idiotic measure." Upon this, the teachers all burst out laughing. "The fault lies entirely with the students. Bad habits will be formed in them if you do not make them apologize to me. Expelling them from school will not be so harsh a measure. What an act of insolence! They made a fool of me as I was a newcomer. ..." Having said this, I resumed my seat. Then the teacher of natural history on my right said that, though the boys were bad, too harsh a punishment would drive them into reaction, and that he agreed with the dean in adopting a mild measure. The teacher of Chinese Classics was also in favor of a lenient measure. The teacher of history was a supporter of Red-shirt, too. Shocking! Mostly partisans of the dean. It would be quite ideal to run a school organized by a company of such personages. I had made up my mind to make the boys apologize to me or else to resign my post; and if Red-shirt got the victory over me I was ready to go home and pack up all my effects. I knew I could hardly vanquish these men in speech, and if I did, it would never do for me to associate with them any longer; their company would be repulsive. I was resolved not to stay in the school, and what did I care, then? They would certainly laugh at me if I spoke again, so I would never say a word more.

Porcupine who had been quietly listening till that moment determinedly stood up. "Man, I know you too are going to support Red-shirt. After all, you and I are enemies. Do as you please. I do not care a pin." This was what I thought, but did not say. Then a loud voice which seemed to shake the glass windows came out of the mouth of Porcupine, who said, "I have on opinion entirely different either from the dean's or the teacher's. From every point of view, it seems to have been an act of contempt and disrespect of the fifty boarders toward the new teacher. My honorable dean was inclined to find the cause of the disturbance in the teacher himself, but might I venture to say, I should think it was a mistake on his part. That teacher had arrived at the school and met the classes only twenty days before he was ordered to be on night duty. No sensible man would think that short period of time was sufficient for the boys to know the teacher and pass a fair judgment upon his character and learning. Were there some reasons justifying their contempt toward the teacher it might not be improper to make some allowance for the boys, but there were no such reasons at all. They simply behaved rudely toward the new teacher in order to make fun of him. If the school, overlooking this plain fact, should let the perfidious boys go free without punishment, the dignity of the school would fall to the ground and be trodden upon. True education, I understand, does not simply help young men to obtain knowledge, but to inspire a noble, sincere, gentlemanly spirit into their whole being so as to drive out wild, perfidious, proud overbearing dispositions from their minds. If, fearing reaction, or that the disturbance would become greater and worse, we adopt a lukewarm measure, these bad practices, I am afraid, will never be destroyed. We are here in

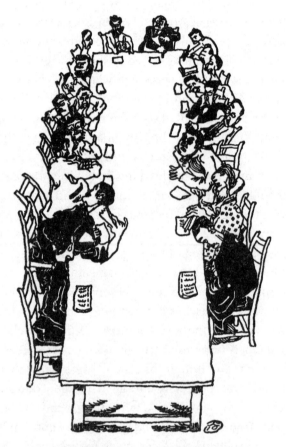

"I have an opinion entirely different either
from the dean's or the teachers'."

this school as teachers in order that we may pull up these corrupt manners by the roots. Were we to overlook this fact, I think we should never have become teachers. The reasons I have been giving above compel me to think it proper to make the boarders one and all apologize publicly in the presence of that teacher to show them how bad they were and how severely they deserve to be punished." Having said this, he resumed his seat with a bump. Nobody said a word. Red-shirt began to polish his amber pipe again. I was greatly pleased; he was, so to speak, my spokesman who said all I had thought to say. I, being such a simple-minded lad, felt very grateful to him, forgetting all the quarrels we had had, and gave a look of thankfulness to Porcupine. He was, however, indifference itself, unconscious of my grateful look.

In a few moments, Porcupine stood up again and said, "Just now I forgot to say a little more; I left it unsaid, and I'll add it. It seems that the teacher on duty that night went out to take a bath at the hot spring. It was an act inexcusable for him to do. Was not he responsible as night watch for the care and safety of the whole school? But seeing there was nobody to stop him, he boldly went out and where do you think he went? Why, the hot spring was the destination of his deliberate choice. It was certainly a great blunder on his part. Although this should have nothing to do with the students' punishment, yet I hope the principal will give admonition to the one who is responsible for this neglect of duty."

Strange fellow! No sooner had he praised me than he tried to make my mistake public. I knew that my predecessor had gone out while on night duty. I thought it was the custom, and so I went out to the hot spring. Now I saw by his remark that I was wrong and that I had no way to defend myself if attacked. Whereupon I stood up again and said that I was wrong to go out to the spring while on night watch; that I was very sorry and humbly begged pardon. On resuming my seat, I was greeted with a volley of laughter from the teachers. "You unworthy fellows!" said I to myself, "Can you frankly confess before the public that you have been wrong! You laugh because you cannot."

Then the principal said that he would take no more of our precious time as he knew that opinions had been exhaustively advanced from every viewpoint, and that he would take necessary steps after careful consideration. By the way, the punishment was that the boarders were forbidden to leave the dormitory for a week; moreover, they had to come out and apologize to me. Had they obstinately refused to do so, I would have resigned and gone home; but as it unfortunately came to pass as I had wished to have it done, a very extraordinary event ensued of which you shall hear afterward. Then the principal, saying it as a part of the meeting, added as follows: "The manners of the boys must be corrected and improved by the good influence of the teachers. As the first step, I should like to ask the teachers not to frequent restaurants save in the case of a farewell party. I should also like to have the practices of going alone to a place of suspicious nature stopped, for instance, a buckwheat, or a dumpling shop and—." He was interrupted in his speech by the teachers' bursting into a great laughter. Noda, the Clown, turning toward Porcupine said "*tempura*" and tried to get response from him by winking, but he paid no attention to his addresses. It served him right!

Having a poor brain, I could not thoroughly follow what the principal said, but if a buckwheat, or a dumpling shop were a forbidden place to go, thought I, such a champion eater as myself would be unable to perform his daily duty as a middle-school teacher. Granting it right, was he just that he had not advertized for a candidate who was not fond of buckwheat or dumpling? No such notice had ever been given; silence had kept it all secret, and now he told me not to do it. Don't you think it an unjust commandment? It was a great blow to me who had no other pleasure to resort to. Then Red-shirt again stood up and said, "Teachers of a middle school, being naturally placed above the level of society, should not always go after material pleasures, for, indulged in, they will have a bad influence upon their character. However, a man not being an angel must have some kind of recreation, or he would be unable to live at such a small place in the country. Therefore, going out fishing, enjoying literature, composing a poem of the new school or an epigram, become a necessity to his existence; in short he should try to find refined pleasure in mental or spiritual pursuit."

Taking advantage of the silence we kept, the proud dean went on speaking as he pleased. Going out into the open sea to catch fertilizer fish; *goruki* becoming Gorki, a Russian man of letters; having his sweet heart, the dancing girl, stand under a pine tree; or composing a poem of seventeen syllables, such as: "A frog plunged into the old pond." (A famous epigram of Basho, the poet.) If these were mental or spiritual recreation it would also be a mental pleasure to eat *tempura* or dumpling. It would be far better and wiser for him to be washing his red-shirt clean than to give an obsolete lecture on an obsolete subject. My anger getting beyond control, I calmly asked him if it was a mental pleasure to meet his Madonna. Nobody laughed this time. Making strange faces, they winked and looked at one another. Red-shirt hung his head as if in great pain. Behold! the sting had gone home to his heart. However, I was very sorry for Mr. Green Squash whose pale face grew paler as he saw I shot the poisonous arrow at the heart of Red-shirt, the dean.

Chapter 7

That very night, I left the room of the house I boarded in. Going home, I began to pack up my things, when the mistress of the house appeared and asked me if there had been anything bad that made me angry; that she would try to amend if I would kindly tell her. Mystery! Wonder! How is the world so full of inconsistencies? Did she really want me to leave her house, or stay in? Conjecture was impossible. It was altogether an act of a lunatic. Had I quarreled with a woman of such mental derangement, the good name of a Yedo man would have been spoiled. So securing a ricksha man, I was out of the house in a minute.

I left the house, but had no prospect of any place where I could stay. The ricksha man asked me where I was going. I simply told him to follow me and that soon he would find out. Thus I was going away in a quick pace, and thought I might go to Yamashiroya, the hotel, as it would save me much trouble. My second thought, however, did not approve the plan, as I should soon have to leave the hotel on account of financial difficulty, and it would make me much more trouble. By walking along in this way, I thought we might find a house with a sign "We take boarders," or some such notice. There I would go in and make my home, believing it a guidance from above. I was going around and around, hunting for a quiet place where I could live in comfort and peace until at last I found myself on blacksmith street, where I knew no boardinghouse could be found as it was a street of samurai residences. I thought of retracing my steps to a more crowded, busier place, when I struck upon a happy idea. Mr. Green Squash whom I respected and loved lived in this street. He was a native of the place, and living in the house inherited from his ancestors. He must be well acquainted with everything in the place. I would go and ask him, and he might be able to find me a good boardinghouse. Fortunately I had called upon him once before, and knew the whereabouts of his residence. It would save me the trouble of hunting. Finding the place where his house stood, I knocked at the door two or three times with "Beg pardon, beg your pardon." An old lady about fifty years of age appeared at the entrance from the back room with an old fashioned paper lantern in her hand. I have no special aversion to a young woman, but whenever I see a respectable old woman, there gushes up in the fount of my heart a feeling of loving kindness approaching veneration. I am so fond of Kiyo, and that spirit perhaps goes over to every old woman found anywhere in the world. I thought the refined old lady with her hair dressed short and trim must be Mr. Green Squash's mother, as they looked so much alike. At the invitation, "Please come in," I told her that I wanted to see him just a moment at the door and would she be pleased to tell him so. Mr. Green Squash soon appearing, I told him all the particulars of the affair and asked him if he happened to know of any home where they took boarders. He greatly sympathized with me and said it must vex me a great deal. He thought about it a while and said, "On the back street, there lives an old couple named Hagino, who told me the other day that as it was useless to have the parlor unoccupied they would be pleased to have a gentleman come and make his home with them, and asked me to find one for them. I do not know if the room is still unoccupied. Let us go and find out." So saying, he kindly took me there.

From that night, I became a boarder with Mr. and Mrs. Hagino. The thing that surprised me most was that so soon as the day following that on which I left Ikagin, the curio dealer, Noda, the Clown, went in and occupied the very room where I had been, with as undisturbed a face as if it were a matter of course. Indifferent as I am, I was amazed beyond measure at this act of brazenness. The world seemed to be composed solely of impostors and schemers who were ever trying to scheme against, and impose upon, one another. Disgusted at this, I got tired of the world; I began to curse life itself.

If such were the ways of the world, I thought, it would never do unless I did as much as the world does. Could I not have three meals a day without the evil money exacted as spoils from pick pockets, it would not be worth while to live in this world, but if I hanged myself while I enjoyed good sound health it would not only contaminate the good memory of my ancestors, but it would also bring disgrace upon myself. The reflection was anything but agreeable. Might it not have been far better to invest that six hundred yen in the milk business than to enter the Physics School and learn mathematics, a learning of little practical use? In that case, Kiyo could have lived with me and I might have been spared the anxiety about her caused from living apart in distant places. So long as we lived together, I did not feel so much of her goodness, but living thus alone in a far country place made me a keen appreciator of her kindness. Go, seek all over the Japanese empire and you will seldom meet with such a good-natured woman as she. The day on which I set out she had a little cold; how was she now? She must have been very glad to get and read the letter I had sent her the other day. It was already time to get an answer from her. Two or three days had been spent with some such line of thought in my mind before I asked the old woman of the house where I boarded in if there was no letter from Tokyo. Often did I ask her and every time she answered, "I am very sorry, but no letter has been received yet."

The old couple here made a great contrast to Ikagin. They were both refined as they were of samurai birth. Every evening the old gentleman sang *utai* (an operatic song) in a peculiar, funny voice, by which I was not a little pestered. But as he did not come in often as the curio dealer did with his usual "Let me serve you tea," I was not so much troubled. The old lady often came into my room and talked over various things. "Why don't you bring your lady down with you and live together?" she once said to me. "Do I look old enough to have a wife? Have pity on me, please, I am yet twenty-four," I answered. "It is natural and proper to have a wife at the age of twenty-four," she replied. With this premise, she went on quoting about half a dozen cases in which Mr. So-and-So of such and such a place, got married when he was twenty; Mr. So-and-So of another place was the father of two children at the age of twenty-two. I was greatly perplexed at this repartee of hers. "Then I shall be glad to have a wife at twenty-four. Will you please find me a good one?" I said using a dialectal phrase or two of her native place. She seemed, however, to doubt the sincerity of my request and asked if I was in earnest.

"Am I in earnest? I am earnestness itself. I want so much to be a bridegroom, and cannot help that."

"Well, that is always the case with young folks. Yes, everybody has had the same experience when young." I was too much taken aback at this frank statement of hers to make an immediate answer.

"But, my young professor," she continued "I am quite sure you are a married man. I know it well. My experienced eye tells me so."

"Well, my old lady, you are quite a clairvoyant. How do you know I have a wife?"

"Nothing simpler, my dear sir. Have you not been so impatient to get a letter from Tokyo? No day passed without your asking me about it."

"Really wonderful! you are indeed endowed with supernatural power."

"Have I not guessed aright?"

"Well—you may be right," was my enigmatical answer.

"But, sir, you must be careful lest you should be betrayed, for young women nowadays are so free."

"Well, do you mean to say that my wife in Tokyo has an unlawful lover?"

"No, your lady is all right, but—."

"Thanks, that puts my heart at ease. What shall I take care about?"

"Certainly she is—Yours is all right."

"Is there any that is not right?"

"We have quite a number here. Sir, do you know that young lady of Toyama's?"

"No, I do not."

"Not yet? She is the most beautiful young lady in this neighborhood. She being such a belle, the teachers of the school all call her Madonna. Haven't you heard of her yet?"

"Yes, I heard of her before, but I thought Madonna was the secret name of a certain dancing girl."

"No, indeed. Don't you know Madonna means a beauty in a foreign tongue?"

"Well, it may mean that; you don't say so."

"I understand it has been given her by the teacher of drawing."

"Did Noda, the Clown, give it to her?"

"Not Noda, but that Prof. Yoshikawa gave it her."

"Is that Madonna bad?"

"Yes, she is bad. That Madonna is not good."

"Good Heavens! No woman having a nickname has ever been good, and it may be so with your Madonna."

"Well, sir, that Miss Madonna had been engaged to—to Mr. Koga, the gentleman who first introduced you to us."

"You don't say so, my old lady. Mysterious is love. I did not even dream that that Mr. Green Squash was so fortunate in a love affair. Indeed, a man's appearance does not tell the whole story; I shall be more watchful."

"Unfortunately Mr. Koga's father died last year. They had been rich and shareholders in several banks; every thing had gone on nicely until that sad time. I do not know how, but Fortune suddenly became very hard upon the family, and it went from bad to worse until poverty stared them in the face. In a word, Mr. Koga, being such a good-natured gentleman, was imposed upon, and the wedding was being postponed by this and that, when the dean appeared on the scene and asked for the hand of Miss Toyama, Madonna."

"Did that Red-shirt really ask for her hand? Rascal! I thought that that shirt was not a shirt of ordinary make. And then?"

"The dean had a parley through a person of his acquaintance with the Toyamas, who, conscious of their injustice to Mr. Koga, could give him no immediate answer, and said they would consider it carefully. He then resorted to other means, was allowed to visit the family often and at last succeeded in obtaining Miss Toyama's love. Mr. Red-shirt was of course wrong, but no less or more blamable was Miss Toyama; everybody criticizes her more severely than him. She had been engaged to Mr. Koga, but when a young B.A. came along and asked for her hand she readily granted his request. The God of today will not approve this act of hers, will he, Sir?"

"It was altogether bad. Not only the God of today, but the God of tomorrow, and the God of the day after tomorrow will all be against her."

"Mr. Hotta was very sorry for his friend, Mr. Koga. He called upon the dean and advised him to discontinue his addresses to Miss Toyama. Mr. Red-shirt then told him that he did not mean to marry a woman who was engaged to another, but he might happen to do so in case the engagement was broken; that he was simply having friendly intercourse with the Toyama family and it could never hurt Mr. Koga's feelings. Mr. Hotta had to come home without any satisfactory result. Messrs. Red-shirt and Hotta are said to be on bad terms ever since."

"My old lady, you seem to know everything. How have you come to know of the particulars of the affair? I am greatly surprised."

"My dear sir, the smallness of this place makes it not only possible, but easy."

Privacy was impossible there; everything was known. My *tempura* and dumpling affairs might be known to the old woman. A troublesome place, yet it was not without some compensation. The meaning of Madonna, and the relation between Porcupine and Red-shirt, became clear and plain. It was a great help for future reference. But what gave me much trouble was the difficulty of knowing which was bad. A simple fellow like myself would be at a loss whose part he should take unless things were defined as black or white distinctly.

"Which is the better man, Red-shirt or Porcupine, my old lady?" I asked.

"Who is Porcupine, I wonder?"

"It is another name for Hotta."

"Mr. Hotta seems of course much stronger, but Mr. Red-shirt, being a B.A., is said to have more power and ability, and to be sweeter to ladies. However, popularity of Mr. Hotta among the boys is greater, I hear."

"In short, which is the better man, I wish to know?"

"In a word, I believe that a drawer of larger salary is a greater man."

Finding no further inquiry was useful, I stopped. Two or three days later, when I came home from school, the old mistress of the house came with a broad smile upon her lips and gave me a letter saying it had long been expected by me and had been received at last; that I should give it a long careful reading. Taking it up after she had left the room, I found it was a letter from Kiyo. It had several small pieces of paper pasted on it, telling that it had first been delivered to Yamashiroya, the hotel, then to Ikagin, the curio dealer, and at last Hagino's. Moreover, it seemed the letter had been detained about a week in Yamashiroya, where travelers as well as letters seemed to find lodging. I opened it and found it to be a very long letter. It ran as follows:—

"My dear Botchan, no sooner had I received your letter than I thought to write you an answer. Unfortunately I had a cold which kept me in bed about a week, hence the delay. Moreover, unlike young ladies nowadays, who are good hands at reading and writing, I had to spend a great deal of time and pains over the letter, poor as the characters I have written are. I thought of asking nephew to write for me, but considering it would never do unless I did it myself, I first wrote a draft and made a nice, clean copy afterward. It took two days to make a fair copy, but four days had been spent over the draft. Doubtless it is a hard letter to read, but as I have taken so great pains to write it, please go through it to the end." With this introduction, the letter about four feet long went on telling one thing and another. It was indeed a hard letter to read. Not only was the penmanship poor, but it was altogether spelt in *hiragana* (cursive characters) with no punctuation marks. Where it began, or where it ended, was impossible to tell, and great pains were taken to punctuate it myself. A reward of five yen would hardly induce me to read such a long hard letter, as I am such a hasty, driving soul. But as it had come from Kiyo, I patiently went through it from beginning to end. Yes, I went through it, but as it took a great deal of pains in going over it, I remembered very little what was in it. So again, I began from the beginning. The room having got a little darker made it a little harder to read, and I at last went out to the edge of the veranda where, with my legs dangled down, I continued to read patiently, when a wind of early fall sprang up; shook the broad leaves of banana plants in the garden; gave its cool breath on my body, and on its return took on its wings the letter I had been intently reading out into the garden to the length of four or more feet with a rustling sound. Had I been poetical enough to let it go, the paper might have flown off to the hedge beyond. How could I be so imaginative at the moment? I was too busy reading the letter. Kiyo went on writing: "My dear Botchan, your character is as straight as an arrow, and I like it, but I am anxious about your quick temper with a word and a blow. Do not give people nicknames, for the act will draw enmity upon yourself. Do stop it, or only let me know by letter if you have had to do it at all. I have been told that the people in the country are bad, so do not be off guard lest you should be cruelly handled. It goes without saying that even the climate down there is worse than it is in Tokyo. Please wrap up your body well with bed clothing when you go to bed, or you will catch cold. Botchan's letter is too short to know about the things over there, and I wish to have at least half as long a letter as the one I have written to you. You did right in giving your landlady a tip, but are you not consequently short of cash? Money is the only thing on which you can rely when in the country, and you

"Do not give people nicknames."

cannot be too economical in order to lay by some for emergency. Fearing your pocket money has run low, I send you a postal order for ten yen. I had the fifty yen you gave me the other day deposited in the P. O. Savings Bank, so that it could be drawn and be a help any time you get back to Tokyo and have a home. I have taken out ten yen, but there still remain forty yen, and it is more than enough, etc., etc." Indeed, woman, thy name is thrift!

I was indulging in deep meditation on the edge of the veranda, the letter from Kiyo flowing out like a pennon in the breeze, when old Mrs. Hagino, opening the paper sliding partition door, came in with my supper. She asked me if I was still reading the letter and said it must be an awfully long one. I told her that as it was a very important letter I had been reading it over and over again, giving the wind full liberty to rustle it. I knew it was not a satisfactory answer to either of us, but I sat at my supper. Behold! the side dish this evening was again the sweet potato cooked with soy. The family of Haginos was far more polite, kind and refined than Ikagins, but one drawback was the poor food they gave me. It was sweet potato the day before yesterday, yesterday, and again this evening. It is true that I had declared I was very fond of potatoes, but if I had to take nothing but potatoes thrice a day, my health would be impaired, and before very long I should be Prof. Pale Sweet Potato and would be laughed at instead of my laughing at Mr. Green Squash. Kiyo on such occasions would give me my favorite dishes, such as tunny (slices *sashimi*), or roasted *kamaboko*. Such luxuries could never be hoped for from such a poor miserly samurai as the Haginos. The more I thought about it, the more desirable it became to live with Kiyo, my old nurse. Were I to stay long here in the school, I would send for her from Tokyo. The buckwheat with fried fish, and sweet dumpling were forbidden and had I to live solely upon potatoes in an obscure boardinghouse, my complexion would certainly get yellow and thin. How hard the lot of an educator would be, I thought. Even an ascetic priest of the Zen sect takes much better food. However, I did ample justice to the plate of potatoes, and taking out two raw eggs from the desk drawer, I broke them on the rim of the rice bowl and ate them. Had I not thus taken nourishment, how could I, with any degree of efficiency, teach twenty-one hours a week?

The letter from Kiyo that day made me quite late in going to the hot spring, but the habit of going there every day for the past few months would make me feel bad if I did not. With my favorite red towel dangling down from my girdle, I proceeded to the station to take the train there. It had started a few minutes before and I had to wait for some time. I sat on the bench and was enjoying a cigarette, when unexpectedly appeared Mr. Green Squash. Mrs. Hagino's talk about him made me feel a greater sympathy with him who was humility itself. Appearing as if he were a parasite between heaven and earth, he was indeed a pitiable object to look upon. A lakeful of tears, however, would never do him any good. I wished, if possible, to double his salary immediately so as to enable him to get married to Miss Toyama that very day and be gone with his bride to Tokyo to spend a month on their honeymoon. Such being the frame of mind I was in, it was quite natural for me to be polite to him. "Are you going to the bath? Please come and be seated." With this, I promptly gave him my seat, which he would not take, humbly asking me not to take so much trouble about him, and kept standing either out of modesty or some such scruple. I repeated the invitation, as he would have to wait some time and get tired. To speak the truth, I really wanted to have him sit beside me; I was so very sorry for him. After much hesitation, he at last yielded to my request, saying it would give me much inconvenience.

There is in the world an obtruder like Noda, the Clown, who will thrust himself upon you uninvited. Porcupine is a fellow who, carrying a proud head on his shoulders, thinks Japan would be placed in a crisis if he were not there. On the other hand, Red-shirt is such a vain fellow who esteems himself the monopolizer of cosmetics and dandyism. Principal Badger thinks himself an incarnation of education dressed in a frockcoat. Each has a world of his own, in which he is king. Never have I met with such a humble soul as Prof. Green Squash, who, like a pawned doll, carries his head so low that nobody takes notice of him. True he has a pale swollen face, but he is such a good gentle soul; no sensible girl save the flirting coquettish Madonna would give him up for Red-shirt. Dozens upon dozens of Red-shirts would never make half so good a husband as he.

"Are you ill? You look quite thin and tired."

"No, I have no special complaint."

"That's good. Illness makes a man useless."

"You look quite strong, sir."

"Yes; I am slender as you see, yet have never been taken ill; I dislike illness so very much."

Some such conversation was being carried on between us, Mr. Squash smiling at my abrupt way of speaking, when we heard a young woman's lively laugh at the entrance. On looking back, whom should we see but a great apparition, a beauty of milky complexion, of high stature, with her hair dressed in fashionable style! An old matron about forty-five was with her; they were seen standing in front of the ticket window. The description of a beautiful woman is beyond my power and I shall not try my hand at it, but a beauty she certainly was. The nice feeling I had at the time was that of holding in my palm a round crystal well steeped in warm, perfumed water. The elder one was of shorter stature, but they looked so much alike, that they must be mother and daughter. From the very moment I felt the presence of the fair lady, I had forgotten all about Mr. Green Squash and had been all attention to her every movement, when all at once he left the seat beside me and approached the young lady and her mother with his usual slow steps. This surprised me not a little as the suspicion she might be Madonna crossed my mind. The three were soon seen before the booking office exchanging formal greetings. Distance made their conversation inaudible.

The clock in the station showed that the train would be starting in five minutes. I got very tired of waiting as I had lost my companion to talk to, and was wishing the train had come sooner, when in came another in a great hurry. It was Red-shirt himself. He was dressed in silk gauze with a crepe girdle slovenly done up around the waist. The gold watch chain as usual kept company with him and peeped out from his belt. The chain was not a genuine one. It was a gilded chain. Presuming all were fools, Red-shirt always tried to show it to the best advantage, but he could not deceive me. No sooner had he come into the waiting room than his sheep's eye was busy looking out for something or somebody. He recognized before the ticket office the three engaged in conversation, went up there, made a polite bow and said two or three nice words. Immediately turning around, he carried his hurrying catlike steps toward me and said, "Are you going to the spring, too? I was afraid of missing the train and came in great haste, but the clock tells we have still a few minutes to wait. I wonder if the clock is right." Then taking out his gold watch, he said that the station clock was two minutes different from his time piece. He sat beside me, but never would he look off toward the woman in question; resting his long chin upon the head of his walking stick, he looked steadfastly right before him. The elderly woman often sent a glance toward Red-Shirt, but the young one would not take her eye off from the spot she first set her glance on. It must be Madonna, I thought.

The train with its whistle came up to the platform. The passengers in the waiting room rushed toward the carriages striving to get in first. Red-shirt was the first to enter the first-class carriage; yet he had nothing to be proud of in going first class, for there was only two sen difference between the two classes. The first-class fare to Sumida was five sen while the third was three sen. So you see two sen made one a first-class man and another a third-class. I myself paid for the first-class and got a white ticket, but my country cousins being economical were very slow to pay the additional two sen and mostly went third-class. After Red-shirt, Madonna and her mother went into the first-class car. Mr. Green Squash was always particular to go third class. It was his stereotyped principle. Standing before the entrance to the popular carriage, he seemed irresolute. However, the moment he saw me approach, he immediately entered that car. Somehow I got very sorry for him and followed him into the carriage. Nobody would think it wrong to get into the third-class car with a first-class ticket.

The hot spring was reached in due time. I went down in my *yukata* (bath attire) from the third story of the hotel to the bath tank where I found Mr. Green Squash again. In a conference, or on some such formal occasion, I become a man of few words as if my throat were choked, but ordinarily I am rather a great talker and I addressed him in the tank, for his sad appearance appealed so pathetically to my sympathy. I believe it is a duty assigned to a Yedo man to cheer up a man in distress with a kind word or two. He, however, was not so ready to dance to the pipe.

Every time I talked to him he simply said "Yes," or "No," and even those words were found to be the result of hard struggle on his part. Thinking it best to discontinue the conversation, I shut my mouth in a minute.

Red-shirt was not found in the tank. As there were so many bathing places, the passengers from the same train were not to be expected to bathe in the same tank and the dean's absence was thought nothing unusual. Coming out of the bathhouse, I was greeted by a beautiful moon. The willow trees planted on both sides of the street were seen casting round shadows of their graceful branches on the ground. "Let me take a little walk," said I to myself. Turning my steps to the north, I reached the bottom of the street where stood a large gate on the left. A Buddhist temple adorned the extremity of the avenue with houses of ill fame on each side. To have brothel quarters inside a temple gate is a unique phenomenon. I wished to enter the gate and have a look, but passed it by lest Principal Badger should find fault with me again. Parallel to it stands a one-storied house with a black curtain and a small lattice window. It was the dumpling-shop where I ate the cake and was punished afterward. A round lantern with the characters *Oshiruko* and *Ozoni* was seen hanging from the shop window. It cast a light which lighted up the trunk of a willow near the eaves of the house. My palate said, "Try." My conscience said, "Don't," and I passed on.

It is hard to have the desire of eating dumpling checked, but harder still would it be to have one's betrothed transfer her love to another. Whenever my heart turned to the case of Mr. Green Squash, I thought taking no dumpling, nay three days' fasting even was a blessing. Indeed, no creature is more treacherous than man. Looking at that Venus-like face, nobody would think it possible for the owner of those beautiful features to do anything heartless. But the contrary was the fact. The fair one was

"It must be Madonna, I thought."

hard hearted, while Mr. Koga, who looked just like a pumpkin distended in water, was the possessor of a gentle, kind heart. Off guard, off head! Porcupine, whom I thought frankness itself, was said to have instigated the boys to make trouble and the very instigator demanded that the principal would punish the boys. Red-shirt, an embodiment of disagreeableness, was much kinder than was expected and indirectly warned me to be on my guard. He was said to have seduced Madonna, and yet he said he would never marry her unless her engagement to Mr. Koga was broken. I thought the man who criticized and drove me out was Ikagin himself, but no sooner had I given up the room than Noda, the Clown, got into it with no scruple. These things made me think nothing on earth was reliable. If I wrote to Kiyo about them, she would be greatly surprised and might say that the place was a den of monsters, as it stood beyond Hakone.

I am careless by nature, and nothing which happened about me had given me any uneasiness, but ever since I came here I have grown conscious of the existence of evils in the world and have become very much alarmed, although I have been here only a month or so. True I had met with no great accident here, yet I felt as if I were older by five or six years. It might be best for me to go back to Tokyo, bidding good-by to such a nasty place, I thought. Thought after thought crossed my mind in rapid succession, until, at last, crossing the stone bridge thrown over the stream I found myself on the opposite bank of the River Nozeri. I said the River Nozeri, but I should be wrong in calling it by such an ambitious name, for it is only a brook about six feet wide with a little bit of water meandering in it. The village Aioi is situated about two blocks below along the banks. The pride of the hamlet is a temple of Kwannon.

On looking back, I noticed red lights shining in the moon light in the town of hot springs. The sounds of drums must be proceeding from the brothel houses. Though shallow, it was a swift stream and the water sparkled nervously in the moonlight. I had been leisurely strolling along the banks and thought I had covered about three blocks, when human shadows were sighted far ahead. The light of the moon showed that they were two. They might be young lads going home to the village from the hot springs. Generally they have a concert of popular songs on going home, but the two before me had none; they were so very quiet.

I walked briskly on and the two shadows grew larger as my gait was quicker than theirs. One of them seemed to be a woman. The distance between the shadows and me was about twenty yards. They heard me approach and the man looked back. The moon was pouring down her rays from behind them. A glance at the man suggested to me the suspicion "Might it not be he?" The two resumed their walk. I followed them at full speed as I had a plan in mind. The two, unconscious of anyone coming after them, were carrying their steps as slowly as before. The conversation between them was now distinctly heard. The dyke was about six feet wide and three could hardly go side by side. I easily overtook them; I touched the sleeve of the man in passing, and went two steps ahead of him. Then turning around on my heels, I looked full into the face of the man. The moon shone right upon my short cut head and down to the chin; she was not polite enough to say "Pardon." A suppressed voice of surprise escaped from the lips of the man. Hastily turning around, he proposed to his fair companion to go back, and they turned their steps toward the town of hot springs. The brazenfaced Red-shirt wished to deceive me, or rather he was too weak hearted to give his name honestly. The smallness of the place, it seems, was not inconvenient to me alone.

Chapter 8

I began to suspect Porcupine after coming home from the fishing excursion to which I had been invited by Red-shirt. When I was told by Porcupine to leave the house where I boarded on a mere pretext, I was confirmed in the belief that he was scoundrel. But on hearing him speak powerfully at the teachers' meeting to punish the boys severely, I thought it strange, for it was quite unexpected. When I heard from the old Mrs. Hagino that Hotta had called on the dean to have a negotiation on behalf of Mr. Green Squash, I clapped my hands in approbation of his gallant action. These circumstances made me feel that Hotta was a good man at heart, and Red-shirt a great rogue, who had indirectly suggested to me unfounded suspicions against Porcupine as if they were true. I had been quite at a loss how to account for these things, when the discovery I made on the banks of the Nozeri, where Red-shirt was taking a walk with Madonna, assured me that he was a great impostor. I was not so sure whether he was a rascal or not, but at any rate I thought he was a bad man—a double-faced suspicious character. Man should be as straight as an arrow, or he could not be trusted. It is a pleasure to fall out with an honest fellow. A man like Red-shirt who appears to be sweet, kindly and refined in his manners and shows his amber pipe proudly must be watched very closely. Pick a quarrel with such a man, and you will reap only regret. I thought that, if I fought him, I could never have such a pleasant fight as we see carried on by wrestlers in the Yekoin Ring. The reflection made me think that Porcupine, with whom I had a hot discussion over that one-and-a-half sen in the faculty room to the amazement of the teachers, was more humane. True I thought him a hateful fellow when he looked at me with his owl-like eyes wide open at the conference, but even that glance was more agreeable than Red-shirt's soft coaxing tone of voice. When the conference was over, I actually spoke to him once or twice in the hope of becoming reconciled with him, but he made no answer and cast a terrible glance at me with his big, round eyes. This made me so angry that I made no further advance toward reconciliation.

Hotta and I had exchanged no word since. The coppers I returned to him were lying innocently on the desk as before. They were all covered with dust. It would never do for me to lay hold of them, nor would Hotta take them. The one-and-a-half sen was, as it were, a bulwark put up between him and me, thus making communication impossible, if I so wished. Porcupine remained obstinately silent. We both suffered from the coppers, so much so that it gave us pain to go to school and look at the cursed money.

While intercourse between Porcupine and myself seemed severed, my relation with Red-shirt was kept up as before on friendly terms. The day after I saw him on the banks of the No-zeri, he came up, sat beside me in a familiar way and asked me how I liked the new home; if I should like to go to fish Russian literature, meaning *goruki*, with him, etc. My feeling toward him now being anything but pleasant, I said to him that I had had the pleasure of seeing him twice the previous night. "Well, at the station?" he said, "Do you always go there about that time? Was it not rather late?" On my telling him that I had also seen him on the banks of the Nozeri, he answered, "I did not go there. I came home immediately after I had a bath." Concealment was useless, for I actually had seen him there. Great deceiver! If such a liar could be dean of a middle school, the presidency of a university I thought would be within my reach. Even after he became an object of distrust to me, I had a talk with Red-shirt whom I did not trust, while I had no word with Porcupine whom I admired. Strange is the way of the world!

One day the dean asked me if I would oblige him by calling on him as he wished to have a talk with me. I thought it a pity to miss a chance of going to the hot spring, but I called at his house about four in the afternoon. Though a bachelor, he had left the boardinghouse long ago and was living in a fine house with a beautiful portico appropriate to the dignified position of dean. The rent was said to be nine-and-a-half yen. If nine-and-a-half yen could supply one with such a fine house in the country, I thought I might also engage a house with a fine porch and make Kiyo happy by sending for her from Tokyo. I knocked at the door with "Pardon," and Red-shirt's younger brother appeared at the entrance. This brother of his was a poor pupil of mine whom I taught algebra and arithmetic. Being a wanderer like a bird of passage, he was far more sophisticated than most of the native country lads.

Meeting Red-shirt, I asked him what he wanted with me. Then smoking tobacco of a vile smell with his favorite amber pipe, he said to me something as follows: "Since your arrival here, better results have become apparent than in your predecessor's time. The principal is very much pleased to have such a good teacher as you. Please do your best as the school authorities place much confidence in you."

"Well, is that so? Do my best? I am doing my very best, and cannot do better," I answered.

"Yes, that is all right. We wish for no more. But please bear in mind what I told you the other day. Do not forget that, pray."

"Do you mean to say that a man who will find another a house to board in is a dangerous character?"

"Be not so outspoken, please, or it will come to mean very little. But that is all right. I know my true spirit is not unknown to you. The school is not blind to your merits and will try to do something for your better treatment. Wait a little longer, and your patience will surely be rewarded."

"Well, is it about my salary? I do not care much about my salary, but I shall be rather glad to have it raised, if it could be done."

"Fortunately, I have one in mind who is to be transferred from this school to another—of course, I can hardly promise you before I consult the principal—and we may be able to draw something from the salary the school has been paying him. I am planning to see and ask the principal to arrange things in that way."

"Thank you very much, and who is going to be transferred?"

"It may be just as well to let you know right now as it will soon be made public. Koga is the man."

"But is not Mr. Koga a native here?"

"Yes, he is, but circumstances compel him to—well, partly out of his own wish."

"Where is he to go?"

"Nobeoka, Hyuga Province. As it is an inconvenient place, he is to go there with better salary."

"Who is to take his place?"

"We already have a man in mind, who comes on such terms as will make your promotion possible."

"Thank you, sir, but I do not care for promotion unless it is right."

"At any rate, I am going to speak to the principal about it; he seems to be of the same opinion as myself, and we may have to ask you to do more work by-and-by. I hope you will be ready to heed our request any time."

"Do you mean to increase my hours?"

"No, the hours you teach may be made less—."

"Fewer hours and more work; it is rather strange."

"It may sound a little strange without further explanation, but the time is not yet ripe to speak out openly. In short, we mean to say that the school may have an opportunity to ask you to take a more important position."

Incomprehensible all this was to me. Red-shirt surely meant by a more responsible position chief teacher of mathematics, which post was being held by Porcupine himself. There was little possibility of his evacuating it. Moreover, it would not be wise policy for the school either to transfer or to dismiss him, for he was very popular among the boys. A kind of fog always hangs over the talk of the dean, but for all the vagueness in his talk, the business part of our interview came to an end. Then a little more time was spent in a chat in the course of which he spoke about a farewell party in honor of Mr. Green Squash, who was a good, lovable gentleman; asked me if I was fond of saké. He went on and on from one topic to another, until at last changing the subject, he asked me if I was a writer of poems. (The reference is to the 17-syllabled poem called *haiku*.) Fearing eternity itself would be too short with Red-shirt, I quickly beat my retreat with, "I am not. Good-by." Basho, the founder of that style of poetry, finds many pupils among master barbers.

A teacher of mathematics would be a laughing stock, if his well bucket were carried away by a morning-glory vender.*

Getting home, I spent a great deal of time in reflection. "It is very strange, I thought, that the world has such an incomprehensible fellow, who, having a house and grounds of his own, says he has got tired of his native place, the school which is very convenient for him to teach in and wishes to go out a stranger to another province in order to meet troubles. Tolerable would it be if it were the flowery capital city where you have electric cars running. What do you think of going to Nobeoka, Hyuga province? A month had hardly passed before I wished to go home, although this place where I am is convenient in water communication. Nobeoka is, I understand, a little town among mountains whose ranges overlap one another. According to Red-shirt, after leaving your ship, you reach Miyazaki by a day's ride in a bus and another day's richsha ride from there will bring you to the place at last. The name itself sounds uncivilized. Monkeys and men may be living there together in equal number. Sage as he is, Mr. Green Squash will not be glad to keep company with baboons, and yet he is going. What a strange choice!"

Some such thought was busy coming and going in my mind, when the old lady of the house came in with my supper. On my asking if it was again potato, she quietly answered that it was *tofu* instead. *Tofu* and potato would make very little difference, though.

"Mrs. Hagino, is it true Mr. Koga is going to Hyuga?"

"Very sorry to hear it is too true."

"Sorry, you don't say so! He goes there of his own choice."

---

* This refers to that famous epigram of Kaga Chiyo, poetess. "Asagao ni tsurube torarete morai mizu." "Early in the morning I went to draw water, and found the bucket with its pole appropriated by the morning-glory flower. I got water at a neighbor's well."

"He goes there willingly? Who?"

"Who, do you ask? Mr. Koga himself. Is it not his own deliberate choice?"

"You are as wrong as wrong can be."

"Am I? But I heard it from Red-shirt himself just now. If it is not true, he must be a devilish impostor, a bundle of lies."

"Mr. Dean may well say that, and Mr. Koga may well say that he does not want to go there."

"Then both seem right. You are always just and fair, my old lady, and I like it. But what on earth are the reasons, I wonder?"

"Mr. Koga's mother came this morning and told me the details of the matter."

"The particulars, if you please."

"Since his father's death, Mr. Koga and his mother have not been so well-to-do as people suppose. They are really in distress, sir. One day, his mother called upon the principal and politely asked him to have her son's salary raised a little as he had been teaching in his school for the past four years."

"Indeed!"

"His mother came home happy with the kind answer of the principal who said he would think about it. The good news from the principal had been waited with great hope. They had waited and waited from month to month until at last Mr. Koga was sent for to call upon the principal. He did so, and was told that the school fund being short he could not manage to raise his salary, but finding a better place in Nobeoka where Mr. Koga could have five yen more a month, he had taken necessary steps to that end, believing it just answered his wish."

"It was a command, and not a consultation."

"Exactly, sir. Mr. Koga was amazed to hear it and asked the principal to let him remain right here as before with the same salary, as he has an old mother and a house of his own. He thought it better than to go to a strange place even if it was with a higher salary. The principal told him, however, that it could not be helped now that necessary steps had been taken and his successor had already been engaged."

"You don't say so! Humbug. Well, I see that Mr. Koga does not wish to go. Naturally I thought it strange. Nobody save a *tohemboku* (fool) would wish to go to that mountainous region in order to keep company with monkeys with a little bit of increase in his salary—only five yen or so."

"What do you mean by *tohemboku*, my dear sir?"

"Don't be so curious, please. It is nonsense. No doubt it was Red-shirt's scheme. It is a deliberate assassination, is it not? And he is bold enough to say he will raise my salary. Let him say what he will, but it shall never be raised."

"Is your salary going to be raised, sir?"

"He says he will raise it, and I am thinking to decline it."

"Why do you refuse it?"

"I will decline it by all means, Madam. That Red-shirt is a great impostor. Base, ignoble coward!"

"However cowardly he may be, sir, you had better accept it like a good boy. While young, one will quickly get angry, but when he reflects upon it as he grows older, he will find to his great regret what a fool he was not to have been a little more patient, but to have become a slave to unprofitable passion. Follow an old woman's advice and accept the dean's offer with thanks."

"Age should never meddle with such a matter. Mind your own business. It is entirely my own concern whether I have my salary raised or not."

The old woman saying no more went away. The old man began to sing *utai* in such an innocent voice as if he knew nothing but bliss in the world. It seems to me that *utai* is an art of obscuring the sense of words by giving them unnecessary, difficult tones when straight reading makes them all plain. An old man who thus idles away night after night with such dull music must be a simpleton, I thought. There was no room in my mind to admit anything like that; it was entirely occupied with another thought. True I consented to have my salary raised, though reluctantly, for I thought it a pity not to spend money when it lay there to be used. Blackmailing, however, should never be my business. I could not be so heartless as to exact a percentage of the salary of the man who was transferred against his wish. What was Red-shirt's motive to order him to go so far down as Nobeoka, when the man in question wished to stay on where he was? Even Sugawara Michizane, an exile, was permitted to find his permanent home near Hakata. Even Kaai Matagoro, an assassin, was to find his safety at Sagara. "At any rate, let me call on the dean immediately and decline his offer right away, or my conscience will never be at rest," I said to myself.

Putting on my cotton *hakama,* I called upon Red-shirt again. I stood at the spacious porch and called out "Pardon." His brother again appeared at the entrance to know what business had brought me there. He gave me such a glance as if my call were a nuisance. I would make a dozen calls if I had business. Midnight even would not be too quiet and sacred a time to knock at his door. I wished to tell the boy that he would make a great mistake if he took me for such a base, servile knave who calls on his dean to pay him homage; that I came in order to decline his brother's offer because I did not wish my salary raised. Being told that the dean had a visitor just then, I said I wished to see his brother a minute at the entrance. The boy went in and left me to look around. A pair of matted clogs of thin delicate shape nicely placed on the stepping stone there caught my eye, and the sound of congratulatory *banzai* from the back parlor reached my sensitive ears. Instinctively I knew

Noda, the Clown, was the caller. Nobody but he could be the possessor of such an affected servile voice, or the wearer of such delicate shaped clogs as are worn by a stage player.

I had not waited long before the dean appeared at the door with a lamp. He invited me to come in, telling me that the visitor was no stranger, but Mr. Yoshikawa himself. I thanked him, but said this place was just as good, for I would not take his time more than five minutes. I noticed his face was flushed and crimson like that of a baboon. The flush came from sake he had been drinking with Noda, the artist.

"Sir, you told me a short time ago that you would raise my salary," I said, "but I have come to decline it, as I have changed my mind."

The astonished dean, holding out the lamp, stared me in the face from behind the light. The abruptness of my remark made him too paralyzed to give me an immediate answer. He thought it strange to see a man who did not wish to have his salary raised, or he thought it was not necessary for him to come back so soon if he must decline the offer at all, or both combined made him dumbfounded. He stood still before me like a statue.

Breaking the ice, I said, "I accepted your offer with the understanding that it was Mr. Koga's free will to be transferred, but . . ."

"Yes, it originated partly from Mr. Koga's wish."

"It is not true. He wishes to stay right on here even with the same salary; he has great attachment to his native place."

"Did you hear it from Mr. Koga himself?"

"No, I did not."

"Who told you then?"

"The old mistress of the house I stay in told me today. She had heard it from Mr. Koga's mother."

"May I understand then that your informer was the old woman of your boardinghouse?"

"Well, yes."

"Pardon me, I think you are a little wrong. If what you say is true, I shall have to understand that you have little confidence in what the dean says, while you accept the old woman's talk like gospel truth."

I was in a dilemma. I thought thus, "A *bungakushi,* being a great man, eats into your flesh like vermin and bites and stings until he gains his point. Father used to say that I was good for nothing as I was so hasty and driving. Indeed, he was right. I had been actuated by impulse on hearing the old woman's talk. I have seen neither Mr. Green Squash nor his mother to hear the particulars of the affair, and when attacked in a bachelor of arts' fashion, I cut a sad figure and was at a loss how to defend myself."

True I had nothing to defend face to face, but I had already passed in my mind a sentence of distrust upon Red-shirt. The old woman of the house I stayed in was indeed miserly and grasping, yet she was not a liar. She was not double faced as the dean was. I answered as follows, as I had no other means to resort to.

"What you tell me may be true, yet, I hope you will please not raise my salary."

"It sounds still more strange. You came here, I understand, to tell me that you were grieved to have your salary raised as you had found reasons for so doing, but your doubts and suspicions have melted away with my explanations, and yet you decline my offer. How can I account for it?"

"It may be hard for you to understand, and yet let me please have my own ways in this affair."

"If it makes you so very unhappy, I shall not urge you to accept it, but I am afraid your future prospects will not be so bright if two or three hours' duration makes your mind change so suddenly without any good reason."

"Well, I shall be responsible for all that."

"You are too unreasonable, my dear friend. Nothing is more important than credit in man. Suppose the landlord of your boardinghouse—."

"Excuse me, it's not the landlord, but the landlady, you mean?"

"Whichever you please. Supposing what the old woman told you be well founded on facts, you will quickly see that what you have gained was no loss on the part of Mr. Koga, who is to go to Nobeoka. His successor comes on lower terms; the surplus goes over to your salary. I see not the slightest point even in the whole matter that will make you uncomfortable. Mr. Koga is to receive better treatment at Nobeoka. The new man comes on a lower salary from the time of contract and you are to go up a little. Nobody is, I think, more favored by Fortune than you, but I shall not try to urge you any more, but will you not think it over once more, please?"

I have not so bright, intelligent a head as I should like to have. Ordinarily such eloquence on the part of my opponent would have convinced me that I was wrong and I should have withdrawn in great confusion from his presence, but it could not have been the case that night. I will tell you why. From the very outset of my coming here, I had an instinctive aversion to Red-shirt. True I began to think of him a little more favorably when he seemed like a kindly woman, but it was only momentary. No sooner had I found that his kindness was not genuine than I began to dislike him as a result of a reaction far more than before. Therefore, however logically he might argue, or however hard he might drive me to the wall in his dignified deanlike fashion, he could not make me believe in him. The man who has had the best of an argument is not always a good man. The man who has got the worst of it is not necessarily a bad man. A superficial observer might have thought the dean right and just in his argument, but he was like unto a whited sepulchre which outwardly appears beautiful. Appearance alone, however attractive, will never make a true lover. If gold, power, or logic could gain a man's heart, a Shylock, a police constable, or a university professor would have the most admirers. However clever a logician the dean of the middle school might be, he could not shake my conviction a bit. Love, not reason, makes man work.

"What you tell me sounds all right, but as I have begun to dislike to have my salary raised, I have nothing further to say than to decline it. Meditation is sure to bring me to the same conclusion. Good-by." With this, I left the house. The milky way above looked down upon me as if to say, "You have done right, boy."

Chapter 9

On the morning of the day on which Mr. Green Squash's farewell party was to be given, I went to school and was unexpectedly greeted by Porcupine who said, "The other day I asked you, you remember, to leave Ikagin's house immediately believing what he had come and told me was true. The curio dealer told me that he did not know what to do with you, as you were so rough and riotous. I took it very seriously but later discovery made it plain that Ikagin is a dishonest fellow who makes it his regular business to sell forged paintings and drawings with forged signatures and seals. What he told me about you must be altogether unfounded. He wanted to get profit by selling you some bad pictures and curios, but as you were too clever to be made a fool, he failed and told that lie. I am very sorry that I did you wrong, not knowing what kind of a man he is, and I must ask your pardon." His apology was long and sincere.

To this, I said nothing, but taking the one-and-a-half sen lying on his desk, I put it back into my purse. Then Porcupine asked me wonderingly if I was really going to put it back into my purse. "Yes," I replied, "at first I did not like the idea of being treated by you and wished to pay, but later consideration has made me think otherwise. I have taken it back as I thought

139

I had better be treated by you." At this, he laughed outright with his usual, loud ha! ha! and asked me why I had not taken it much sooner. I answered I had wished to do so often, but the bashfulness I felt compelled me to let it lie; that of late it made me feel quite ill at ease to come to school and see the coppers. "You are a man who knows no defeat," said he, "or knowing, does not admit it." "You are quite stiff necked, too," was my repartee. The following conversation was then carried on between him and me.

"What is your native place?"

"I am a Yedo man by birth."

"Exactly. That's why I thought you were so proud and self-sufficient."

"Where do you come from?"

"From Aizu."

"From Aizu? Well, I see. Stubbornness is a characteristic trait of Aizu people. Will you go to the farewell party today?"

"Certainly I will, and you?"

"Of course, you shall see me there. I am even thinking to go down to the port to see Mr. Koga off."

"A farewell party is great fun. You must come today to see me drink heavily."

"Well, you may take as much as you will, but I'll come home immediately after I have eaten up all the dishes served. A fool is a thirsty soul!"

"You are ever ready to pick a quarrel; you are a typical Yedo man who is fickle, excitable—a man of hasty hot type."

"Enough! Enough! Will you please drop in at my lodging place before you go to the farewell party? I have something to tell you."

Porcupine called at my home punctually at the appointed time. I had felt very sorry to see the sad face of Mr. Green

Squash ever since I knew of his soul-gnawing disappointment. At last the day of the farewell party had arrived. My sympathy with him grew to such pathos as I thought I might go to Nobeoka instead, if such an arrangement could be made. He was so pitiable an object. I therefore wished very much to stand up and make a speech over the dinner in order to give Mr. Koga a prosperus God-speed, but my light flippant Tokyo dialect would never do. Porcupine would be, I thought, the very man to perform this important task, for he had such strong lungs. His loud voice would surely frighten the dean to death, hence his call at my lodging.

I started out with the Madonna affair, and of course Porcupine knew about the intrigue much better than I. I extended my talk to the secret meeting of the lovers on the banks of the Nozeri and said that Red-shirt was a fool. He was rather offended at this remark of mine and said that I had a very bad habit of calling everybody a fool, that he had been called so at school that morning; that if he were a fool, Red-shirt could not be one, for he was not of the same stuff as he. At this I corrected my mistake by giving the dean another appelation far worse, "worthless dunce," and he was very much pleased with this, saying it was just splendid. Strong as he was, Porcupine's vocabulary in such matters was far poorer than mine. May be Aizu people are all of the same stock.

The raising of my salary and his promise of giving me a more important post were the things I next told him about, to which he gave a single "pooh!" through the nostrils of his big nose, and said that Red-shirt was planning to put him out. "Are you ready to resign even if the dean asks you to?" I inquired. "No, not I," he proudly answered. "He shall go with me when I am dismissed." Being asked how he could manage to do that, he answered he had not thought about it yet. Favored as he was with great animal vigor, he had little share of wisdom. On my telling him that I had declined Red-shirt's offer to raise my salary, he was very much pleased and praised me saying, "Genuine Yedo man, you are truly worthy of the proud name."

On my inquiring why he had not offered his services to enable Koga to stay right on in his present position as he was so unwilling to go to his new place, Porcupine said that it was too late when he heard of it, yet he called on the principal twice and the dean once to negotiate, but all in vain, for it was after the arrangements had all been made. He continued that Mr. Koga being too good a man, was quite helpless in the matter; that he ought to have given a decisive refusal outright, or at least should have asked the dean to let him have a little time to think it over when the proposition had been made by him, but having consented on the spot, deceived by his smooth tongue, neither his mother's petitions with tears, nor his frequent calls had the slightest effect. He was sorry about it.

I said that it was the dean's scheme to gain Madonna's love by sending away Mr. Green Squash. "Exactly!" said he, "He is such a rascal as to affect innocence, while hatching up some bad plan, and when his villainy is exposed, he defends himself with plausible excuses ready at his beck. 'Dealing with the fist' is the only way that will tell upon such a scoundrel." Saying this, he rolled up his sleeves and showed me his arm full of muscle lumps. By the way, I asked him if he was a good hand at jujitsu as he had such strong arms. Upon this, Porcupine, making a stonelike prominence on his arm by the biceps-flexor muscle told me just to squeeze it. I felt it with my finger tip and it was exactly like the pumice stone used at the public bath.

Out of admiration, I said that he with such big arms could easily knock down half a dozen Red-shirts at a time. "Of course I can," said he and began to move his arm out and in, so that the stonelike muscle lump in the skin moved to and fro like a pendulum. It was so very interesting. According to his own statement, he could easily break a pretty thick twisted paper thread tied around the muscle lump. The thread would be off in a second when he bent his arm with one, two, three. "Well," said I, "I think I can with a paper thread." "No, never," he said, "Try if you could." Thinking failure would invite contempt, I stopped.

"Have you no great mind to give a good shake to Red-shirt and Noda, the Clown, at the farewell party tonight after the liquor has permeated all through your system?" I jokingly suggested to Porcupine, who seemed to hang a moment on the suggestion, and then said he would not do it that night. I asked why. "Mr. Koga would be placed in an awkward position if I did," he said, "moreover, unless I thrash them in the very act of their villainy if I do it at all, I shall be blamed." He added that a wise man would never do that. It seems that even he thought himself more discreet than I.

"Would you then make a speech in which you will commend Mr. Koga highly?" said I. "My Tokyo dialect will never do on such an occasion, for light and smooth as it is, it lacks in power. Moreover, whenever I appear before a public audience, I am strangely attacked by a fit of pyrosis, which sending something like a big ball up the throat almost chokes its passage, hence my asking you to take up the task" "It is a strange malady," he said. "You are then unable to speak in public at all, is it not very inconvenient?" "No, not very," I answered.

In the meanwhile, the appointed time arrived. Porcupine and I went together to the place of meeting. It was a restaurant named Kwashintei the best of the kind in the place, I heard. I had never been there before. The proprietor of the restaurant had purchased the house from the chief retainer of the daimyo there, and remodeled it into the present accommodations.

There he opened his restaurant business. Indeed, the outward appearance of the restaurant was quite imposing. The manor house of a chief retainer transformed into a restaurant is something like underwear made of a military coat.

On our arrival, we found that almost all the members of the faculty had come, and forming two or three groups in the fifty-mat hall were gossiping away the time. The alcove of the room was proportionately big; it being so large, that of Yamashiroya's fifteen-mat room I once occupied seemed very poor in comparison. It measured twelve feet in width. A porcelain vase with vermilion patterns was ceremoniously placed on the right of the alcove. A big branch of a pine tree was found arranged in it. I could hardly understand why they had put a pine branch in the vase, but the idea came no doubt from the economical point of view, as it would never fade, but be ever green month after month. I asked the teacher of natural history where that *setomono* came from and was answered that it was not a *setomono*,* but an *imari*.* "Is not *imari setomono*, too?" I said and he simply smiled in derision. Later information made it plain that they call earthenware *setomono* (Seto things) as it is manufactured at Seto, Owari Province. I, being a Yedo man, thought all porcelain *setomono*. A large hanging scroll was seen hung against the wall of the alcove. It had twenty-eight big characters, each character being as big as my head. The hand writing was so poor that I asked the teacher of Chinese Classics why they had so shamelessly put up such a scroll with such ugly characters, and was told that they were scripts written by a famous penman named Nukina Kaioku. Were it Kaioku or not, I still think they were very poor penmanship.

---

* Seto and Imari are the names of places where porcelain is manufactured, and the former is used to cover all kinds of earthenware.

At the request of Kawamura, the clerk, to be seated, I took a seat just in front of the pillar against which I could lean back whenever I wanted. Principal Badger in his *haori-hakama* sat with the hanging scroll of Kaioku at his back, in the honor seat; on his left sat Red-shirt also in *haori-hakama,* while on his right was seated Mr. Green Squash, the guest of honor of the night. He was also dressed in Japanese ceremonial dress. My foreign clothes made me feel so very uncomfortable that I sat down right away with my legs crossed, but the teacher of gymnastics in his black trousers next to me was particular to sit on his heels. I dare say his calling made him behave so punctual strictly according to the rules of etiquette. In due time, all the individual tables with dishes on were set and wine bottles were placed ready to be drained. The teacher who presided stood up and gave a brief opening address. He was followed by Principal Badger. Lastly Red-shirt spoke. They were unanimous in commending Mr. Koga in their farewell speeches. They said that, as he was such a good teacher and a fine gentleman, they were very sorry to lose him from among them; that it was a great loss not only to the school, but also to them as individuals; however it would be unjust for them to detain him as he had so earnestly wished to be transferred for his personal convenience. This was an utter lie, but they were so shameless as to give Mr. Koga a farewell party. Of the three, Red-shirt was most profuse in flattering words; he said in the course of his speech that it was the greatest misfortune for him to lose such a good friend. His way of speaking was so sincere in all appearances and his voice was so sweet that anybody who had never heard him before would have been completely taken in. He must certainly have won Madonna's hand with the same trick. In the midst of the dean's farewell speech, Porcupine who sat opposite winked at me with lightning speed and I put my thumb on my nose in response.

Red-shirt had hardly resumed his seat before Porcupine stood up to speak. Unconsciously I clapped my hands, as it gave me great satisfaction. Upon, this, Principal Badger as well as the rest of the faculty focused their glances on me, so that I felt a little perplexed. I was, however, all attention to hear what Porcupine had to say. He said, "The principal and other gentlemen, especially the dean, expressed their great sorrow at Mr. Koga's removal to another post, but I have a different opinion; I find no reason to be sorry about it. On the contrary, it is my earnest desire that he will lose no time in leaving this place; a day's delay will make him more uncomfortable. Nobeoka being a small out-of-the-way town among mountains may not be so convenient on the material side as this place. According to the information I have obtained, however, the people there seem to be very primitive and simple in their customs and manners; teachers and students seem to retain honest simplicity handed down from time memorial. I believe there is no such sweet-tongued high-collar hypocrite who gives you complimentary remarks out of hypocrisy, and for all his handsome countenance tries to entrap a good honest man in order to advance his own personal interests. Hearty welcome of the people there is, I am sure, awaiting you, a gentleman of so good and noble a character. I therefore have the greatest pleasure in congratulating Mr. Koga on his removal this time. I must add before I close that he will, on his arrival at Nobeoka, choose an accomplished lady fit to be the life companion of a true gentleman, and establish an ideal home at his earliest convenience, so as to give spiritual death to that inconstant, faithless coquette." Making two or three coughs at the close of his speech, he resumed his seat. I wished to give him a hearty cheer again this time, but did not lest the people in the room should stare me in the face to my great discomfort. Porcupine's resuming his seat was the signal for Mr. Green Squash to stand up in response. He was so polite as to leave his own seat and go to the end of the room. After giving all present the nicest bow, he proceeded to say that he was going to Kyushu for his personal convenience and he was very grateful to be given a splendid farewell dinner by all the teachers; that he would conscientiously try to follow the good words expressed by the principal, the dean, and other gentlemen. He concluded by wishing that they would be so kind as to keep him in their favor in future as in the past, although the distance between them was great. He bowed low again and went back to his seat. Nobody could sound how deep down his goodness lay. He was politely thanking the principal and the dean who had been making a fool of him, and his gratitude did not seem to come simply out of his lips, but from the depth of his honest heart. This was quite plain from his appearance, his way of speaking and the expression of his face. A man who has an ordinary share of conscience will surely be ashamed to have such sincere thanks from such an honest man; but it was not so either with Badger or with Red-shirt. They were just listening to him with assumed profound gravity.

No sooner had the speech making come to an end than sipping sounds here and there were heard coming out of thirsty throats. I did not take sake, but had a sip or two of the soup, following the example set by others; it was awfully unpalatable. On the dessert plate was found a big piece of *kamaboko* (hashed fish seasoned with a little sake and salt baked on a piece of wood). It looked so very disagreeably black just like a spoiled *chikuwa* (the roughest kind of *kamaboko).* *Sashimi* (raw fish cut in thin slices, usually eaten with soy) was also served, but the pieces were so big and thick that one might think he was eating raw tunny in ugly steaks. However, my neighbors right and left were seen doing ample justice to these dishes with great relish.

I dare say they had never tasted things cooked in the style of good old Yedo.

In the meanwhile, bottles of warmed sake had been busily passing from hand to hand, and good cheer reigned in the whole room. Respectfully approaching the principal before all others, Noda, the Clown, was drinking to his health in a servile manner. A disgusting fellow! Mr. Green Squash was going around and drinking to the health of each of the teachers in turn. I should think it was a nerve-straining task on the part of Mr. Koga. At last he came around to me, and, arranging the folds of his *hakama* according to the strict rules of etiquette, he sat and politely asked me to give him leave to drink to my health. Uncomfortable as it was, I sat on my heels with my trousers on and returned his toast. I told him that I was sorry to part with him so soon after I arrived there. I asked when he was leaving and added that I would go down to the beach to see him off. He politely declined my offer saying I was so busy and need not come down. Nevertheless, I had made up my mind to go and give him a hearty God-speed even if I should have to stay away from school that day.

In an hour's time, disorder began to have its sway in the room; liquor had done its intoxicating work. One or two had thick sticky tongues so as to make their words indistinct. "Man, a glass. I command you drink," one was saying to somebody, or rather to himself. Being a little bored, I went downstairs to wash my hands; there the old-fashioned garden caught my weary eye; gleams of twinkling misty stars gave it the primitive serenity of the great past. Porcupine had also found his way down there and suddenly addressed me with, "How did you like that speech of mine, was it not awfully fine?" He was in high spirits. I answered that it was just splendid with one exception which was not to my taste. "What was that?" he inquired.

"Well, did you not say there is no such sweet-tongued, high-collar hypocrite at Nobeoka who will push down a good man into the pit?" I replied.

"Yes, I did."

"High-collar hypocrite was not enough."

"What should I have said then?"

"High-collar hypocrite, swindler, impostor, rogue, juggler, mongrel, detective, snarling cur."

"Indeed, I have no such smooth tongue. You are so fluent. You have so rich a vocabulary. Wonder why you cannot make a speech."

"Well, they are the stock words I resort to in the time of a quarrel. In speech making, they won't come so easy."

"Won't they? I wonder how you could command such a long list of words. Will you not try it once more, please?"

"Yes, with pleasure, as often as you please. One, two, three! high-collar knave, swindler, impostor, hyp. . . ." I was interrupted by a stamping sound made by two or three who came staggering along the long corridor.

"You two, too bad. Playing truant? No, you can't, never! while we are here. Come and drink. Impostor! That's very good. Come and get drunk."

With this, the two liquor slaves were dragging Porcupine and me with what strength they had. Apparently they had come to wash their hands too, but being tipsy they forgot and were hauling us upstairs instead. It seems that a drunkard forgets everything in his mind so soon as he finds a new opportunity arise before his swimming eyes.

"Gen'lemen, I've brought the impostor. Give him drink. Give it in full until he gets drunk, this swindler. Man, don't try to run away!" And he pressed me hard against the wall, although I did not try to escape. Looking around, I found every table had been cleared, no dish remained whole. Some there were who, having eaten up all their own, had gone on an expedition ten or twelve yards beyond. Principal Badger was no more to be seen; he had probably made his sly exit.

"Pardon, can we come in?" Some three or four dancing girls with their *shamisen* came into the room. I was not a little surprised, but being hard pressed against the wall I could do nothing but stare vacantly at this strange apparition. Immediately after the singers came in, Red-shirt who, with his back against the alcove pillar, had been proudly smoking his favorite amber pipe, stood up suddenly and was about to leave the room, when one of the girls smiled him a greeting as she passed in. She was the youngest and the prettiest. Distance made her salutation inaudible, but she must have said, "Good evening, my sweet gentleman, so glad to see you." The proud dean affected ignorance and passed out of sight never to make his appearance again that night. I dare say he followed the principal and went home.

The dancing girls brought sunshine with them into the room, and all welcomed them with lusty cheers; so loud and noisy were the cheers as if they were raising war cries. Some took the opportunity to start the game of odd and even. The shouts "odd?" or "even?" they uttered were just like those of a juggler practicing his sword feat. Some here playing *ken* throwing in ejaculations Yo! Ha! with such earnestness and skill as Jeanne D'Arc and her men could do no better with their puppets. Some there in the corner were shouting, "Serve us sake, girl!" but finding the bottle empty, they corrected their mistake by telling them to fetch more wine. I was bored to death by the din and confusion caused by those revelers. Mr. Green Squash was the only sober figure among them; and he with his head down was brooding over the dark prospects lying before him; he had nothing else to do. They declared that it was the farewell

"Good evening, my sweet gentleman, so glad to see you."

dinner given in his honor, as they were extremely sorry to part with him, but it was not true; they held it simply because they wanted to have a jolly time at his expense. Mr. Koga was the sole sufferer from the riotous revels he could not enjoy. One would be only too glad to be given no such farewell dinner.

In a little while, each began to sing his favorite ditty with as much noise as he could command. The dancing girl who came and sat before me asked me if I cared to sing; taking up her *shamisen* she was ready to play the accompaniment. I told her I did not care to sing, but she should. She began singing,

> With drum and bell, Santaro,
> A lost child, was searched for,
> Dondoko dongno chanchikirin!
> I too have a man I long to search
> And meet with drum and bell.
> Dondoko dongno chanchikirin!

She sang it in two breaths and said it tired her all out. Why didn't she sing a much easier one, if it was so hard, I wonder?

Before anybody noticed it, Noda, the Clown, had come and was sitting by the side of the singer whom he addressed as Suzu-chan. "Miss Suzu," he said, "You see your lover only to see him out. I'm too sorry to say so." His way of punning was, as usual, just like that of a professional storyteller. The girl, putting on a serious air, answered, "I do not know, sir." Determined to pursue the game, Noda, the Clown, sang out, "Prayer being heard, I saw him, but—"* in a disagreeable bass after a musical drama player. The girl slapped him on the lap with "Won't you

---

* The passage is from a famous drama "Asagao Nikki," the pathetic love story of a blind girl.

stop?" The artist was so much pleased with the slap as to draw out a broad smile on his lips. She was the girl that had greeted Red-shirt as he passed out. Noda must be a sweet indulgent ladies' man to be pleased with the slap of a dancing girl. "Miss Suzu," he said, "I wish to dance *Kiinokuni* (a popular folk song) to your *shamisen*, won't you please oblige me?" It seemed that he wanted to dance, too, not content with flirting with the girl.

Yonder sat the old teacher of Chinese Classics, who was heard singing with his twisted, toothless mouth, "That's not fair, Dembei-San! Man and wife have we been; you and I—."* Thus far he was right, but stopped short to ask the singer what followed. Poor memory seems to be the universal trait of an old man. One of the girls, taking hold of the teacher of natural history, was asking if he cared to listen to a ballad then very popular, and she began to sing it to her *shamisen* telling him to be all attention. "Dressed in European style with a white ribbon, her hair is so fashionably nice. She rides on a bike; she plays on the violin. Her half-mastered English serves her purpose well and she says 'I am glad to see you.'" The song pleased the naturalist so much as to draw out admiration from him. "It is so wonderfully fine; it has English," he said.

Porcupine in a very loud voice was shouting, "Girl! girl! I'm going to do the sword dance. Come and play the accompaniment." The girls, greatly taken aback at his extraordinary outcry did not know what to do. Porcupine, caring not a pin for the tardy girls, proceeded to dance. Advancing to the midst of the room with a heavy stick which served for a sword he began to dance to the heroic song,†

---

* A musical drama.
† The poem was composed by Rai Miki, the son of the great historian, Rai Sanyo.

Peak after peak with fleecy clouds I have trodden with my sandaled feet.

It was his hobby and he was riding it to his heart's content. Then there appeared a rival dancer on the scene. Noda, the Clown, having exhausted all his dancing skill in *Kiinokuni, Kappore*, and *Dharma on the shelf* came with a palm broom under his arm and began to march up and down the room shouting out the war ballad which begins with "Rupture of Sino-Japanese negotiations." He had no clothes on except a small piece of cloth around his loins. Inmate of a madhouse!

I felt very sorry for Mr. Green Squash, who had been sitting painfully on his heels still with his *hakama* on. I thought he had no need to sit still and look on in his ceremonial suit at the ugly naked dance, even though the dinner was said to have been given in his honor. So I went up to him and urged him to go home, but the honest Squash would not stir an inch, saying it would not be just right for him to leave before the rest as it had been given in his honor. He politely asked me to go ahead. "Don't worry about it, my friend," said I, "It is not the right kind of a farewell party. See those madmen's ugly pranks. It is nothing but a madman's meeting. Come, let us go."

Unwillingly Mr. Koga rose as I persistingly urged, and we were just coming out of the room, when Noda, the Clown, wielding his broom, came up and said that it was impolite for the guest of honor to leave before the rest; that it was a Sino-Japanese negotiation; that he could not let him go. With this, he blocked the way by holding his broom crosswise. My pent-up anger now burst out with tremendous force. "Sino-Japanese negotiation? Then you must be a Chinese devil," I cried and gave him a hard blow over the head with my fist. Two or three seconds had passed before the amazed artist found his mouth. "This is pretty hard. It's a pity you have beaten me. You have struck me, this Yoshikawa. Much obliged! This is a real Sino-Japanese negotiation." He was spinning out a yarn which made no special sense, when Porcupine, who knew there was some commotion down below gave up his sword dance and came striding to the scene. The sight irritated his nerves so very much that he took hold of Noda's collar and gave him a sudden pull. "Sino-Japanese; ouch! ouch! What violence!" escaped from the lips of the Clown, who tried to free himself from the Titanic grip. Porcupine gave him a twist, and down he fell with a heavy bang. What followed I did not know. I parted from Mr. Green Squash on the way and got home. The clock on the wall struck twelve.

Chapter 10

The celebration of victory won by our troops over in China gave us a holiday. Various exercises were to be held on the Parade Ground. Principal Badger with the students had to go and attend. I, as one of the faculty, had to go with them, too. The streets were all so beautifully bannered with the Rising Sun flags as to dazzle the eye. Headed by the teachers of physical exercise, the eight hundred students were to go there in a long line of procession. The line was divided into companies with a little space between. This space was to be filled by a teacher or two as leader. The plan itself was very fine, but how to carry it out successfully was quite another matter. Besides being naughty, the boys were also impertinent and seemed to think it an honor to disobey the rules of discipline, and no matter how many teachers might go with them, it was of very little use. They would yell out any war song they chose before they were told to, and would raise a lusty war cry at the end of each song. They were, so to speak, outlaws tramping along the streets. When they had no war song, or raised no war whoop, they would be chatting loudly as they trudged on. One would reasonably think that they might walk without being talkative, but, the Japanese being born talkers, no admonition could make them keep still.

Chatting itself would be quite inoffensive, but when the chatterer begins to give many bad names to another, it becomes base and offensive. I thought myself perfectly safe from scandalous names, as the boys had given me a nice apology in the night-watch affair, but no; the fact showed me that it was a mere illusion. To borrow the phraseology of the old woman in whose home I stayed, I was wrong as wrong could be. Their apology did not come out of true repentance; they formally bowed their heads down before me simply because they were told by the principal to do so. Trade people are very obsequious, but never cease to be dishonest in order to make profit. So it was with the students; they would apologize as often as they had to, but never would they give up mischief-doing. Reflection was anything but pleasing. The world seems to be composed of such persons as the boys. A man comes and apologizes to you, saying he is sorry he has done you wrong. You give him full pardon honestly believing it true repentance and you are made a fool. So you will be quite near the mark to think that he comes to you to ask forgiveness just for the sake of appearance, and you pretend to excuse him for the same reason. Do you truly wish to lead him into true repentance? You can do it only when you beat him down into contrition.

As I walked on with the boys in the space allotted between companies, confused sounds of "*Tempura*" or "dumpling" constantly reached my ears. Nobody could tell from whom it proceeded, for there were so many. Even if it were known whom it came from, the perpetrator would shamelessly tell you that he did not call you "Fry" or "dumpling," but that your nervousness made you so suspicious as to imagine it was meant for you. This mean, base, ignoble trait, a relic of the feudal system, growing to be the second nature of the people in this place could not be eradicated either by persuasion or by preaching. Innocent as I

"Confused sounds of *"tempura"* or "dumpling"
constantly reached my ears."

was, I might have to imitate their evil ways, if I stayed here a year or so. No good dice player would tolerate it if you tried to cheat him by some dishonest means, from which you could escape when caught. Two can play at the game. If they were men, I was no less so. Whether students or boys, they were far bigger than I as far as bodies were concerned, and some kind of revenge must be inflicted as punishment for sheer justice's sake. However, if you adopted some ordinary method of revenge, they would turn around, snarl at and bite you. If told they were bad, they would eloquently insist upon their innocence as all sorts of excuses had been prepared beforehand. Thus making themselves apparently justified, they would turn their poisonous tongues and attack you mercilessly. As you did it for retaliation, your vindication would avail nothing unless it brought their evil doings to light. They first sowed the seeds of evil, but after all you would reap the result of being looked upon as the real cause of the quarrel. Nothing would be more disadvantageous than this. If on the other hand, you played the part of an idiot and let them have their own way, they would behave themselves as they pleased. The world would greatly suffer if such were tolerated. Therefore, knowing it wrong, you would have, out of necessity, to adopt their method and return like for like in such a stealthy way as to give them no chance to pounce upon you. If you came to that state of degeneration you would be no more a Yedo man than a crow a crane. I feared it would bring me down to that stage of degradation, yet, being a man, I should have to compromise my conscience to circumstances, and be a vile, base, despicable being in the course of a year or two. These reflections made me think that the only way to save me from this spiritual peril was to return to Tokyo right away and have a home with Kiyo, my old faithful nurse. "Stay in the country no longer," my conscience seemed to say, "It is far better to be a newsboy than to go down so low."

I had been carrying my unwilling steps with these unpleasant thoughts, when a commotion and bustle in the van caught my attentive ears, and the procession came to a sudden stand. Thinking it strange, I left the line on the right and looked toward where the noise came from. At the foot of Ohta street where Yakushi street branches off, I saw a confused mass of people contending to get ahead, pushing on and pushed back. A gymnastics teacher came along, shouting at the top of his hoarse voice, telling the boys to behave better. On asking what the matter was, I was told that the middle school and the normal school came to a collision at the corner.

A middle school and a normal school in any prefecture are, I am told, on bad terms. Nobody can tell why, probably the difference of *esprit de corps*. They are like a dog and a monkey. They will fall out whenever chance makes them meet. This is perhaps one of their ways of killing time which hangs heavily upon their hands, as the social circle of the country is so very limited. Being fond of fight, I ran as fast as I could toward the place where they had run against each other, partly out of curiosity and partly to have some fun. "Make way, you local taxes,* make way!" shouted those in front. "Push, push!" shouted back those behind. Elbowing the boys in the way, I was just coming out into the corner, when a loud sharp command, "Right face, boys! March!" was heard and the normal school students began to march in good order. The contention as to which should be the first seemed to have come to a mutual understanding, and this was brought about by the middle school yielding a step. The normal school is said to be above the middle school in educational standing.

---

* Middle schools are maintained with local taxes, while normal schools are supported through the national treasury.

The exercises at the Parade Ground were brevity itself. The commander of the army corps read a congratulatory address; it was followed by that of the prefectural governor; the assembled audience all shouted "Banzai." That was all. As the program of entertainment was to be given in the afternoon, I went home and began to write Kiyo an answer which I had long had in mind to write. She had written to ask me to send her a long letter with fuller details, and I had to do as she had asked. But when I took up the paper, I found I did not know where to begin, as I had so many things to write. "Will that do? Yes; but it makes me too much trouble," thought I. "Will this do? Yes; but it is dull. Is there not something which coming out so smoothly gives me no pains and yet makes Kiyo happy to read?" It seemed quite plain that no such thing ever existed. I rubbed the ink stick on the stone ink box, dipped the writing brush in the ink and gave a steady glance at the rolled paper—I stared at the paper, dipped the brush in the ink and rubbed the ink stick on the stone. I went through the same process over and over again, until at last I found I could not write a letter, however hard I might try. Disappointment made me put back the lid of the ink box. I thought it gave me great pains with little result to try to write a letter and it would be a great deal quicker and better to go back to Tokyo and see Kiyo, and have a personal talk with her. She would certainly be waiting anxiously for my letter, but to write a letter as she had wished me to was more painful to me than to fast three weeks.

Putting aside the brush and letter paper, I lay down on the matted floor, making a pillow of my arm and began to look down into the garden, but my heart still turned upon my old nurse. Then I thought thus, "I live far away from her, yet she and her welfare are the theme upon which my heart constantly dwells. My true heart will reach her on the wings of morning.

If so, there will be no need of sending her a letter. If there is no letter, she will think that her young master is safe and sound, for sickness, death, or some such accident only will necessitate correspondence of any kind."

The garden of about ten *tsubo* was a mere flat patch of ground with no specially good trees, but it boasted one orange tree. It was so high above the fence that it was a sort of landmark to the passers-by. This tree was my favorite and I looked at it whenever I came home. To me who had never left Tokyo before, an orange tree with many oranges was a rarity. Those green balls ripening day by day would soon turn yellow and look very beautiful; some of them even then had already got a yellow tint. The old lady of the house told me that the fruit was sweet and juicy, and that when it was ripe, I could help myself to it as much as I wished.

"Yes, the fruit shall be my comfort every day," I thought, "Three weeks more, and the oranges will be ripe enough to satisfy my palate. It is not probable that I shall have to leave this place within twenty-one days."

My thoughts had been occupied with the orange, when Mr. Porcupine called. It was an unexpected pleasure. He said that as it was a Red Letter Day, he had brought some beef to eat with me. Taking out a bamboo-sheaf wrapper from his sleeve, he placed it in the middle of the room. I was very glad to have it, for potatoes and *tofu* had been the diet my stomach had been persecuted with in the house where I stayed. Moreover, the buckwheat and the dumpling shops had been forbidden places and the meat he brought was very welcome to me. I lost no time in borrowing a pan with a little sugar and soy of the old lady and began to cook it.

Porcupine, greedily helping himself to the beef, asked me if I knew that Red-shirt had a dancing-girl sweetheart. "Of course, I know," I answered, "Is it not one of those who came at the time of Green Squash's farewell meeting?" "Yes, that is the one. I am surprised at your shrewdness," Porcupine was pleased to say, "I have known it only recently."

"Refined character or spiritual pleasure is Red-shirt's favorite topic on which he always dwells at length," Porcupine said, "but he is such a rascal as to have intimate relations with a dancing girl. He would not be so blamable if he were lenient toward others. Was it not he who through the lips of the principal gave you warning that it was injurious in keeping up good discipline of the boys to go into a buckwheat shop or to a dumpling stand?"

"Yes," I said, "Red-shirt seems to think that flirting with a *geisha* is a spiritual pleasure, while to taste *tempura* or dumpling is a gross material enjoyment. If so, he himself should do it openly. But shame on him! No sooner had his intimate *geisha* come in than he left the seat and ran home stealthily. He is such a brazen-faced knave as to try to deceive people by his knavery. If attacked, he will tell you he does not know, or call it Russian belle lettres, or that short poem and the new school poetry are twin sisters, and so forth. He always tries to express his opinions in such a way as to mystify his opponent. Noble manhood will be spoiled by such a weakling. He is so effeminate that everybody thinks him a metamorphosis of a court lady's maid. Perhaps his father was a *kagema* at Yushima."

"What do you mean by *kagema*?"

"A fellow who is womanish. Man, don't eat from that part of the pan; the meat there is still raw. A tapeworm will find good food in your stomach if you take raw meat."

"Well, I think it is cooked enough. I have been told that the dean goes secretly to the hot springs and there meets his dancing girl at Kadoya."

"Is Kadoya a hotel?"

"Yes, it is a hotel and restaurant as well. There I will watch and catch him when he comes with her and I will cross-examine him in the presence of the girl. This seems to be the best way to humiliate Red-shirt."

"Do you then mean to 'catch him' by keeping night watch?"

"Yes; you remember there is a hotel named Masuya just opposite Kadoya. We'll rent the front room upstairs, and there we shall be watching through a hole in the paper door."

"Will he come when we are on watch?"

"Yes, I think he will. Of course, you can hardly expect success in a night or two. We shall have to watch at least a fortnight."

"Well, it will tire us all out. I remember I sat up till dawn and nursed father on his death bed. It was only a week; still it made me so dull that I could hardly do anything afterward."

"I do not care if it does affect me a little. If he is overlooked, such a scoundrel as he will hatch up many schemes detrimental to the interests of Japan, and I have made up my mind to chastise him in the name of Heaven."

"Splendid! If things are settled that way, I shall be delighted to stand by you through thick and thin. Are you ready to begin your night watch tonight?"

"No, that cannot be, for I have not seen the master of Masuya yet."

"When do you expect to begin?"

"Before very long, you may be sure, and I will let you know when everything is ready. I can count upon your aid?"

"Yes, certainly. I shall be ready to assist you any time. I am rather a poor strategist, but when it comes to actual engagement, depend upon it, I am quite a good fighter."

Porcupine and I had been busily consulting over the beef pan how the chastisement of Red-shirt could be carried out, when the old lady of the house came and told us that a student of the school had come and wished to see Prof. Hotta. She said that the student had been to his house, but finding he was out, he had come around, rightly guessing he could find Mr. Hotta here. Kneeling at the threshold, she waited for his answer. With "Yes, I'll see him," he went out to the door, and, returning in a minute, said that the student had come to take him to the entertainment ground where a certain dance peculiar to Kōchi Prefecture was to be performed by a great number of men who had come for that purpose. He insisted upon my going with him, as the dance was said, as he added, to be a rare sight. He was very anxious to go and see it, and he urged me to go, too. No kind of dance was attraction to me, for I had seen so many in Tokyo. Each year at the festival of Hachiman Shrine, I had a chance to see all sorts of dances performed on the movable stage drawn about from street to street by oxen. Therefore, *Shiokumi* and all other dances were no novelty to me, and I had no great desire to go and see the vulgar dances of those rustic cousins from Tosa Province; but thinking it impolite on my part to decline Porcupine's urgent invitation, I went out with him to the gate. Red-shirt's younger brother was the student who had come to fetch Porcupine to the fête. O that he were somebody else!

On entering the place of entertainment, we saw many long flags or pennons whose poles were planted in different parts of the place. Besides, the place was adorned with festoons of flags suspended from nook to corner; the air was alive with so many beautiful flags that one might think they had been borrowed from all the nationalities of the world. At the eastern corner of the place, they had built a temporary stage where that peculiar dance of Tosa was to be danced. About half a block from the stage on the right we found an exhibition of flower arrangement in a booth of rush blinds. All were admiringly looking at the different schools of that art. My artistic instinct was shocked to see it. How is it that people are so pleased to see plants and bamboos persecuted, some bent, some straightened? They might as well be proud of having a hunchbacked lover, or a lame husband.

In the opposite direction, fireworks were being set off. The rocket bursting out in midair let out a balloon with the characters, "Long live the Empire!" which, floating lightly over the tapering pine tree by the watch tower of the castle, fell at last behind the barracks. Bang! another went up like a big black dumpling, and it seemed as if it were going to pierce through the autumn sky. Bursting above my head, its blue smoke spread out like so many ribs of an umbrella and slowly faded away into the air. Another balloon was set off. This one had the characters, "Long live the Army and Navy!" They were white on the crimson background. The wind bore it away, away to the town of the hot springs, and thence to Aioi Village. Maybe it fell on the temple grounds of the goddess *Kwannon*.

The ceremonial part of the exercises in the morning was not attended by so many, but the afternoon witnessed a great concourse of people. I was surprised to see so many come out. I did not think that the country was so thickly populated. Though there were only a few intelligent faces, yet numerically the crowd was not one to be slighted. In the meantime, that outlandish dance of *Kochi*, which had aroused so much popular excitement, was being performed. I had thought that the dance was something like that performed by Fujima, dancing master, or some such thing, and I was greatly disappointed.

Three rows of men were formed on the stage, each composed of ten men in short *hakama* with white linen bands tied round their heads. What surprised me most was that every one of them was armed with a drawn sword. The space between the front line and the back line was no more than fifteen inches with equal or shorter space for each dancer on the right and left. Apart from the rows, there stood a man at the corner of the stage, who had on a *hakama*, but no headgear, and in the place of a drawn sword had a drum suspended from his neck. The drum was exactly like that of *daikagura*[*] both in size and shape. "Ya! Ha!" came out of the throat of the conductor, who began to drawl out some funny song in a dull sleepy voice. In order to mark time, the beating of his drum was kept up and "pokopon, pokopon" went on with the dance. I had never heard such a strange air before. It would be no great mistake to think it a kind of mixture of "Mikawamanzai"[†] and "Fudaraku."[‡]

Like liquid *ame*, in midsummer, the dull song was drawled out to eternity, but the "pokopon" coming in, in time, served to keep it in tune, no matter how long it might be drawn out. To this music, the thirty men danced, so many blades flashing like lightning. The skill and quickness of motion made the spectators almost shiver with fear. Right and left, before and behind, you have your neighbors within fifteen inches, and they as well as you brandish their sharp swords as they dance. Unless it be done with skill and harmony, you will get hurt by fighting with one another among yourselves. If your neighbors simply flourished their swords right and left, up and down, without moving themselves, it might not be so dangerous, but the thirty in a body would turn sideways, turn around in a circle, or bend their knees, beating time with their feet on the floor. Were your neighbor a second too soon or too late, you might have your

---

[*] A dance performed in the street by men wearing wooden lionheads.

[†] Strolling comic musicians and dancers who go about from house to house at the beginning of the New Year.

[‡] A pilgrim who goes about from house to house singing a melancholy hymn marking time with a little tinkling bell.

nose cut off, or your neighbor might have his head sliced. The blades were brandished without the least restraint, but as their movement was confined to the square space of one-and-a-half feet, it would never do, unless your sword were waved in the same direction with the same speed as your neighbors right, left, before and behind. It was indeed a wonderful feat. Truly no such dances as *Shiokumi* or *Sekinoto* could equal it. I was told that it requires great skill on the part of dancers to keep pace with one another. The hardest part, however, is said to be that of the conductor with the drum, drawling out that peculiar tune; his "pokopon" seems to regulate all the movements of hands, feet, and the beating of knees of the thirty dancers. Onlookers might think him getting most fun with the least pains, for he looks such an easygoing fellow with his exclamations, "Iyah!" "Ha!" Strange to say, he seems to be playing the most difficult part of all, and his responsibility the greatest.

Porcupine and I had been looking at the dance with wonder and admiration, when all at once a war cry was raised about half a block away from where we stood. The crowd that had been leisurely looking at so many exhibitions and shows began to move right and left like a great wave. Hardly had we heard the shouts, "Fight! Fight!" when Red-shirt's brother came running threading his way through the concourse of people. "Fight again, sir," said he out of breath, "The middle school, you remember, was disgraced by the normal school this morning. Our boys wanted to get revenge on the latter, and a fight has just begun. Please come and help us, quick." With this, he left us and disappeared among the crowd.

"The naughty boys have again come to blows," said Porcupine, "Compromise seems to be an unknown virtue to them." With this, he ran as fast as he could toward where the fight was going on, making his way through the throng who were fleeing in all directions. Probably he could not well look upon it with indifference and had gone to put it down if he could. I had no more mind to run away from it than Porcupine himself. Following him at full speed, I appeared soon upon the scene. The fight was now at its height. The normal-school lads were about sixty; the number of the middle-school boys was larger by thirty percent. The former all had on uniforms; the latter were all in Japanese clothes, as they had changed clothes after the ceremony in the morning. A distinct line therefore could be easily drawn between friends and foes, yet as they were jostling, jumbling, driving on, or being driven back in great confusion, neither of us knew what to do in parting them. Porcupine, who had been looking at the whirlpool of blows and kicks with a look of dismay, intimated to me that we could do nothing, but to plunge into the heat of the fight to stop it if we could, before the police came to interfere. I gave him no answer, but plunged right into the thickest and fiercest part of the strife. "Stop! Stop! young rascals, or your schools will be disgraced. Won't you come to reason?" cried I, and tried to get through what seemed to be the boundary line of friends and foes, but all in vain. Four or five yards in, I found myself like a poor fly caught in a spider's web. A normal-school boy, a comparatively big fellow, seizing hold of a middle-school boy, some fifteen years old, was shaking him violently. "Did I not tell you to stop, blockhead?" said I, and holding him by the shoulder, I tried to tear him off the younger boy, when somebody (how could I know who he was?) mowed my feet from under me. This sudden blow made me tumble down sideways, letting go my hold of the shoulder of the other fellow. The hard soles of boots were felt on my back. I sprang up immediately on both my hands and knees. The fellow on my back, with his hard boots, rolled down on my right. Again finding me upon my feet, I saw some six yards away the big body of Porcupine wedged in among the contending boys. He was shouting at the top of his voice, "You boys, stop. Stop your fighting, won't you?" as he was jostled and shaken by the human tide. I told him that it was no use any longer to try to stop it. He gave me no answer. I dare say my message did not reach his ears.

A stone came whizzing through the air and hit me right in the cheek bone. No sooner had I felt it than down came the hard blow of a club upon my back. "Aren't they teachers? Books ought to be their recreation. Beat them, strike them!" said a voice. "They are two; a big one and a little one. Throw stones at them," cried out another. "Away with your impertinence! you savage rustics!" I cried, and struck the normal-school boy I held over the head. Another stone came whizzing through the air and grazing my short-clipped hair flew far back from where I stood. What had become of Porcupine? He was to be seen nowhere. "A blow for a blow! True I came first to put down the fight, but where is such an idiot as to run away trembling after he is beaten and stoned?" I thought. "Who do you think I am? Short as I am in stature, I am your elder as far as fighting goes. My special training along that line in its headquarters proves it," I cried and pell-mell I hit out and was hit back. Thus the fighting was going on when the cry "Police! Police! fly!" was heard and with the shout I found myself much relieved, as both friends and enemies had all taken to their heels. Before this, I had been struggling, as it were, through a pond of jelly, so hard pressed and jammed in had I been in the throng. Escape was accomplished by the boys so quickly and skillfully that it was doubted if General Kropatkin even could have made such a masterly retreat!

How did Porcupine fare in the engagement? He had his un-lined *haori* with his family crest on badly torn, and was seen wiping with his handkerchief his nose which was bleeding from the blows it had received. It was ugly to look at his red swollen nose. I had on a lined garment of *Kasuri* pattern, but it was not in half so bad a shape as Porcupine's, though it was much smeared with mud. My cheek, however, began to ache almost unbearably. Porcupine told me that my face was still bleeding pretty freely.

When the police, sixteen in all, came to the scene, the boys had all run away in different directions, and we were the only ones left behind, whom they could get hold of. We gave them our names and the details of all that had happened. However, they wished us to go to the police station with them; so we did. After describing to the head of the station all we knew, we were free to go back to our boardinghouses.

Chapter 11

O n awaking next morning, I found I had pain all over my body, limbs and all. As I had been out of practice for a long time, the fight of the preceding night seemed to have heavily taxed my nerves and energy. This humbled me so much that I thought I could boast no longer of my hardiness in fight. Thus musing, I was still in bed greatly crest fallen, when the old woman of the house brought the "*Shikoku Daily*" and placed it at my bed side. The newspaper was no attraction to me that morning, so tired and discouraged was I, but thinking it would never do for a man to be disheartened by such a trifling event, I took courage, and lying flat on my belly, I began to look over the paper, when behold! my eyes rested upon an article on the second page. It was an account of the quarrel of the previous night. It was quite natural to find it in the daily, but what disgusted me most was the libel about us. It ran something like this: "Two of the faculty of the middle school, one, a certain Hotta; the other, an impertinent fellow So-and-So, just fresh and green from Tokyo, set on the good students to fight. They not only led and directed the boys in the field, but also were so bold as to personally attack normal school students." It went on to say, "The middle school of the prefecture had been looked up to as the model of good well-ordered *esprit de corps*, but now that that time-honored reputation had been so mercilessly destroyed by these two rascals to the disgrace of the whole community of the city, we could not but take the matter in our hands in order to investigate where the responsibility lay. We believe, however, the authorities concerned will speedily take necessary measures before we do to inflict such severe punishment upon them as to make them unable to appear in the educational world again." Every word was italicized to call the special attention of the reader. Thus the poor pressmen of the local paper thought that they had applied to us the hot moxa (had punished us). "Damn it!" cried I and sprang out of bed in an instant. Wonderful to say, the pain I had felt in the joints was so greatly alleviated that I forgot it as soon as I left my bed.

Tearing the paper in pieces, I deliberately made a ball and threw it into the yard. This, however, did not satisfy me until I took it to the dirt-hole. A newspaper is an organ for fabricating and telling lies. Nothing in the world is so great a liar as a newspaper. The *"Shikoku Daily"* printed all I myself should have said. What an instance of rudeness to say an insolent fellow So-and-So, fresh and green from Tokyo! "Is there anybody under the sun whose name is So-and-So? Come to your senses, man," thought I. "Say you wish to know my name, and you shall know mine is as fine as any. If you want to see my family line you shall see it with every one of my great ancestors down from Tada Mitsunaka himself." Immediately after my morning toilet, I felt a sudden pain in the cheek. The old lady of the house brought me a looking glass on my asking, and inquired if I had looked over the paper. I told her that I had, and had thrown it away into the dirt-hole; that she had better pick it out of there if she wanted it. She went back much amazed. A look in the mirror showed me as many ugly scratches as there were yesterday. Unattractive as my face is, it is as important as any, and that organ had been badly wounded. Moreover, I was called an impertinent fellow So-and-So. Indeed, it was more than I could stand.

Thinking it a disgrace beyond remedy if it was thought that I stayed away from school because I was intimidated by the newspaper article, I took a hasty breakfast and was the first to attend school. One after another, those who came in had a smile at my face. What made them smile, I should like to know. My face had not been made by them, and I owed them nothing. In the meanwhile, Noda, the Clown, having come into the room said to me, "A great achievement yesterday! Aren't they the wounds of glorious victory?" He might have thought it revenge for the blow I had dealt him at the farewell party. His sarcastic tone irritated me beyond control. "It's none of your business," cried I. "Mind your own paint brush!" At this, he was sorry he had said it and begged my pardon. However, he added that it must be painful, nevertheless. "Whether it is painful or not," exclaimed I angrily, "it is my own face, and you need not meddle with it." Silently he went away to his own seat farther off where he and his neighbor, teacher of history, casting frequent glances at me, began to talk in a whisper with ironical smiles upon their lips.

Then there appeared Porcupine with his nose swollen up so purple that pus would gush out if it was pressed. Self-conceit made me feel that his face had fared far worse than mine. Being neighbors in the teachers' room, Porcupine and I had our desks side by side, which, unfortunately facing the entrance to the room, disclosed our two sorry faces to every comer. All darted glances at us whenever weariness bored them. They unanimously said it was an unfortunate event and were sorry with their lips, but they must have thought us fools in their minds, or they would never have laughed at us in their sleeves, all the time whispering something with one another. Cheers awaited us in the classrooms. "Long live, master." Hurrah!" some two or

"The desks unfortunately facing the entrance to the room, disclosed
our two sorry faces to every comer."

three shouted out. But I did not know whether it was meant for applause or irony. While Porcupine and I were thus the focus of attention, Red-shirt alone came to us as usual, and said he was very sorry for us, and he had seen and consulted the principal about sending the paper a correction, and we need not worry about it. He was sorry that his brother was the cause of all the trouble, for, he said, if his brother had not invited Mr. Hotta out, the trouble would never have occurred. He went on to say that he was extremely sorry and he would spare no effort in order to settle it to our satisfaction. His words were partly sympathetic and partly apologetic. The principal came to our room from his in the third period and expressed a pessimistic view about the affair. He anxiously said what the paper wrote had greatly troubled him and hoped it would turn out nothing serious. On my part, I had no anxiety whatever. If they wished to dismiss me, I would defeat their stratagem and resign before they were aware of my intention. However, if I resigned conscious of my innocence, it would help make the vicious paper more vicious, and I made up my mind to make the paper correct its mistake and to remain in the school right on. On my way home, I wished to call upon the newspaper office, but stopped as I was told that the school had already taken necessary steps to have the report corrected.

Porcupine and I explained to both the principal and the dean when they were not engaged, all that had actually happened. They both said that what had been described by us was true; that the newspaper entertaining an ill will toward the school had manufactured and put that malignant article in the paper. After that, Red-shirt was seen going around the room telling all one by one that Mr. Hotta and I had done just what was to be done, and declaring that it was his own fault that his brother had invited Mr. Hotta out. The teachers one and all seemed convinced that the blame lay entirely in the paper and it was indeed a calamity to us.

On our way home, Porcupine warned me to be on guard lest Red-shirt should betray us. "Well," said I, "that he is a suspicious character has long been known, and it is no surprise to find him so now." "Don't you see," he remarked, "that we fell into his snare yesterday when he led us out into the midst of that fight?" Indeed, my sagacity did not go so deep down. Hasty as he appeared, Porcupine was, I thought, far cleverer than I.

"Thus he led us into the fight and secretly supplied the paper with material to write that malicious report. He is such a villain."

"Is the paper another Red-shirt then? It is really surprising, but will the paper so readily accept what Red-shirt has to say?"

"Yes, it will. It is simplicity itself, when you have a friend there in the office."

"Has he a friend there?"

"It could be done even if he had none. You tell them a lie and say it is a whole truth, and they will directly print it in their paper."

"You don't say so! If it is Red-shirt's trick we may be dismissed before very long in connection with this affair."

"When fate is against us, we may be turned out any moment."

"If that is the case, I will send in my resignation tomorrow and go back to Tokyo right away. I would not stay a day longer even if they petitioned me to stay."

"The dean will not suffer a bit if you should resign."

"Well, indeed! How can we make him suffer?"

"Such a ruffian as Red-shirt takes too great precautions to give one a chance to discover evidences against villainy, and it is awfully hard to catch him."

"Indeed! And they will blame us as false witnesses. It is something very disagreeable. Is Heaven just, I wonder?"

"Let us wait a few days longer to see what will come. It won't be too late to resort to the last resort when every other possible means has been exhausted, that is to say, to catch him at the town of hot springs."

"Laying the quarrel affair on the table?"

"Yes; and strike him on his vital spot."

"Well, let it work. I am a poor strategist and I rely entirely upon your wisdom. I will do anything when needed, I assure you."

After the dialogue just recorded, Porcupine and I parted. The dean must indeed be a villain if he had done what Hotta imagined. Wisdom would prevail very little over such a knave, for he is far cleverer than we; force would be the only means to confute him. Truly it will be long before cursed war will be swept away from the surface of the earth, for force seems to be the final court of appeal even in the private affairs between man and man.

Next morning, the paper impatiently waited for was at last delivered. I searched and searched for the correction or any such thing all over the paper, but all in vain. Going to school, I demanded of the principal how it was. He simply replied that it would appear in the following day's issue, and so it did. It had the correction the school had sent in in small pica, but the apology it should have made could be found nowhere. Again I asked the principal why it was so. Then he said he could not do anything more; that it was all that could be done. A principal having a face like that of a badger, and wearing a suit of frockcoat like a dignitary, is merely a figurehead, having very little power and influence. And the principal in question was no exception to the rule. He failed to make a poor country paper apologize for its false statement. This made me so angry that I told him I myself would go and see the editor about it. "No, it will not do," said he, "It will simply make the matter worse, for your visit will make him still more cross and he will write a worse libel about you. Once you are written about, you cannot do anything with it, be it false or otherwise, and you will have to resign yourself to it as fate has it." It sounded altogether like the preaching of a priest. If a newspaper were such a nuisance, it would be a great benefit to humanity at large to do without it. I did not know before the principal's explanation that to be written about by a paper and to be bitten by a snapping turtle are the same in result, no remedy for either.

Three days had passed before I was called upon one afternoon by Porcupine, who seemed much agitated. He said he had made up his mind to resort to the last measure we had talked about, as the time was ripe. I told him I would follow his example and join in the plot. He was, however, not so ready to accept my offer, but shaking his head said I had better not do it. I asked him why I should not; then he inquired of me if I had been told by the principal to resign. "No, not yet," I answered and added if he had been. "Yes," he said, "The principal called me in and told me today that he was sorry, but could not but ask me to leave school on account of unavoidable circumstances."

"That is an unjust judgment, as unfair as could be. The Badger has beaten his belly-drum too hard and the bowels are probably upside down. Don't you remember that you and I attended the victory celebration together, we both saw that sword dance and we two plunged into the heat of the quarrel to stop it? A just principal would have told us both to send in our resignations together. What a blockhead is the head of a country school! Provoking, is it not?"

"Red-shirt is, so to speak, the man behind the gun. He and I cannot get along together under the complicated circumstances, but he thinks you will be no harm to him if you remain here right on."

"But, I will not go with him. It is impudence itself to presume I shall be so harmless to him."

"You are so simple, and he thinks he can manage you as he pleases."

"Worse and worse. Others may work together with him, but I cannot, I will not."

"Moreover, the man who is to take Koga's place after he was gone some days ago has not come yet owing to some unaccountable circumstances. In addition to this, if they were to lose both of us at one time, there would arise a great difficulty in arranging the schedule, as many gaps in the lessons would naturally be formed."

"Then they mean to make a wedge of me, and just put me in for the time being, and then bid me good-by. Two can play at the game, I should like to tell them."

Next day, I attended school as usual and lost no time in going into the principal's room.

"Sir, why did you not tell me to resign, too?" I demanded.

"What!" he said and stared me in the face in great astonishment.

"Is there any law that tells Hotta to resign and me to stay right on?"

"To suit the convenience of the school."

"There you are wrong. If I need not give up my position, I hardly see why Hotta has to."

"I can hardly explain it to you now, my dear Mr. B. We'll have to bear the loss of Mr. Hotta, but we see no necessity for your resignation."

Indeed, the appellation of a badger seemed to be the most appropriate in his case, I thought. He went around and around and evaded coming to the point and yet he was so self-possessed. Thinking it no use to argue with him any longer, I jumped to the point all at once.

"Then I will resign, too. Do you think I can remain in my present position in peace and let Hotta go alone? I can never be so heartless."

"Pray do not do that. We shall find ourselves in a great fix if you do that. Mr. Hotta goes and you go; the boys will have no lessons in mathematics."

"I cannot help that."

"Do not be so persistent in having your own way, my dear Mr. B. Be more sympathetic with the school if you please. You have not been here a month yet; if you leave us now, it will be disadvantageous to your future career. I think you would better think about that point a little more carefully."

"I don't care about my career. To do my duty by a friend is first and last."

"Yes, you are right. What you say is all true, and I admire you for it, but I earnestly hope you will please lend your ear to what I ask you. If you are determined to resign, we shall have to acquiesce in it, but please stay here until we have found your substitute. At any rate, will you please think it over again at home?"

The reason of my leaving the school was so plain that there was no room for reconsideration, but as Principal Badger turned red and pale alternately, I felt a little sorry for him and left his room, saying I would think it over again. Neither a word of greeting nor of scorn did I address to Red-shirt, on whom I thought it far better to inflict severe punishment once and for all for so many crimes he had perpetrated, if I were to punish him at all.

When I told Porcupine all the details of my conversation with Badger, he said he had thought that something of the sort would be the result, and added that it would not be so inconvenient for us in carrying out our prearranged plan, even if I should put off my resignation till the time was ripe. I followed his advice. He seemed much cleverer than I, and I made up my mind to do whatever he advised me to do.

At last Porcupine sent in his resignation; bade adieu to all the teachers and went down to Minatoya, the hotel at the beach. But secretly coming back, he got into the upstairs front room of Masuya in the town of hot springs, and there he began his maneuver of looking out through the hole he had made in the paper sliding door of the room. Nobody save myself knew anything of the matter. Night would be the only convenient time to enable Red-shirt to come incognito; early evening would invite many students and other folks out to disturb his secrecy, and at the earliest, nine P.M. would be the time for him to sally forth without being noticed. The first two nights I kept watch till about one A.M. Not a shadow of Red-shirt could be seen. On the third night, I sat up from nine to ten-thirty and all to no purpose. Nothing is so foolish for one as to tramp at the dead of night all the way home without seeing even a glimpse of success. Four days had hardly passed before the landlady of the house I boarded with began to be a little uneasy about my late behavior and advised me not to go out at night as it would make my wife in Tokyo miserable. I told her that mine was not an ordinary nocturnal excursion of the sort she feared, but an expedition to chastise a certain ruffian whom Heaven should have punished. However, a full week's experiment bringing no satisfactory result, I naturally got very much discouraged. Though driving and hasty, I can sit up working till dawn when I get enthusiastic, but that zeal never lasts long in any undertaking I try my hands on. Heaven commissioned chastizer as I was, I began to grow tired of the monotonous job. The sixth night brought me no encouragement. I thought of staying away on the seventh evening. But Porcupine was obstinacy itself. He would, from early evening till past midnight, apply his sharp eye to the paper door and through the hole stare at the ground beneath the round gate lamp of Kadoya, the restaurant. Every time I went in, he would give me statistics of the total number of visitors the restaurant had that day; the number of those who stayed over night, and the number of dancing girls who came and went, etc., were minutely given. It was indeed miraculous. At my discouraging words, "I am afraid he will not come," he would tell me that Red-shirt would certainly come, and folding his arms, the poor fellow would often heave a long sigh. Unless the dean were now gracious enough to appear once within the range of his eye, Porcupine would be unable to inflict his Heaven-commissioned chastizement upon Red-shirt all through his life time.

The eighth evening found me out of the house I stayed in at seven. After taking a long comfortable bath, I came out into the street and bought eight eggs in order to make up the want of nourishment from the potatoes of each meal which the old mistress of the house incessantly served. Carrying four eggs in each pocket with my favorite red towel on my shoulder and both my hands in my pockets, I went up the staircase of Masuya and opened the paper door of the room where Porcupine sat watching. His Goliath-like face all of a sudden beaming with hope greeted me. He had looked quite blue till the night before, and I had felt very sorry for him, who carried something gloomy and melancholy about him, but now seeing his face brighten with expectation, my heart was so much cheered up that I shouted "banzai" out of the happiness I felt even before I heard anything from Porcupine himself.

"That dancing girl named Kosuzu went into Kadoya about half-past seven this evening."

"With Red-shirt?"

"No____."

"Then it is no use."

"The girls were two; they came together. It seems quite promising."

"How?"

"Well, he is, you know, such a sly old fox. He may have sent his girl before him and plans to follow her afterward incognito."

"Yes, it looks like that. Is it not nine yet?"

"Yes, it is a quarter past nine," said he, and taking out the nickel watch he was carrying in his belt, requested me to put out the lamp right away lest the sly fox of the dean should get suspicious by noticing the two big shadows of our heads cast upon the paper door.

The lamp placed on the small light table was immediately put out, but a little light still hovered on the shōji as the stars began to appear, although the moon was not risen yet. Porcupine and I with our faces close to the door waited and waited stealthily until the clock on the wall struck nine-thirty.

"Will he come at all? In case he won't come tonight, I will give it up."

"But I will never give it up until my fund has run short."

"How much have you left?"

"I have paid up to this day five yen and sixty sen for eight days' rent. I pay the rent each night so as to cause me no inconvenience whenever I have to leave."

"You are preparedness itself. Surely you are a surprise to the hotel keeper and his people."

"No, they are not so much alarmed at my strange behavior, but that which troubles me most is that I can hardly leave my eye from the hole on the shōji."

"You take a day nap, do you not?"

"Yes, I do. But confinement in the house day and night all but kills me."

"Great pains are what we have to endure in order to give him a Heaven-commissioned punishment. They say that Heaven's net, however big the meshes may be, is sure to catch the wicked. But if it should fail and the wicked should escape, nothing would be more disappointing."

"Do not be so pessimistic; he will certainly come tonight.— Look! there he comes."

His voice lowered into a whisper and my heart leapt with a bound. A man with a black hat looked up at the gate lamp of the restaurant and passed out of sight into the dark. It was not Redshirt. Disappointment stared us in the face. In the meantime, the clock behind the counter struck ten as a matter of course. The night seemed to fail us again.

Time wore on; stillness began to reign all around. The drums played in the houses of ill fame were very distinctly heard. The street beneath was lighted by the moon, which, with her beautiful pale face, had risen from behind the hill of hot springs. Then were heard human voices toward the foot of the street. Who were the owners of the voices could not yet be ascertained, for it would have been foolishness itself to put out our heads from the window, but they seemed to come nearer and nearer, as the clatter, clatter of their clogs gradually grew audible. Looking sideway through the hole, we could see two shadows approaching. "We are safe at last; those in our way have been driven away." This certainly came out of the lips of Noda, the flatterer. "Brutal force with very little share of wisdom is to be pitied," came from Red-shirt. "That swearer is an interesting character; he is such a hasty, driving, simple boy; there is a charm about him," continued Noda, "He declined to have his salary raised; he wished to send in his resignation; sure he is beside himself." I would have broken open the window, jumped down from upstairs and beaten them flat on the ground, but controlled myself with no small difficulty. The dean and the artist with their usual Aha! Ha! passing from under the gate lamp disappeared into Kadoya, the hotel.

"Well."

"Well?"

"Here they are!"

"Yes, at last."

"I am so happy now."

"The brute of Noda said I was a headstrong, driving, simple boy."

"They referred to me when they spoke of one in their way. Impudent rascals!"

Porcupine and I wished to take them by surprise on their return home, but when they would come out of the saloon nobody could tell. Porcupine, going downstairs, asked them to leave the door unlocked, as business might suddenly call us out even at midnight. It is a wonder to think how they agreed to his request. In all probability, they might have thought us burglars.

It was hard for us to wait for Red-shirt to come to the restaurant; still harder was it to wait for him to come out of it. It would never do for me to go to bed, leaving Porcupine alone, yet keeping on staring through the crevice of the shōji was a great tax upon my nerves. Getting unaccountably impatient and restless, I had never felt such a painful sensation before. I proposed to break into Kadoya and catch them right in the midst of their carouse. A word of Porcupine put my proposition to naught. He said that we should certainly be interrupted as housebreakers if we broke into the house; that they would tell us there were no such persons in the house, or they would show us into another room even if we gave them reasons to interview them; that if we could break in unawares, it would be impossible to tell the room where they were from so many sets of rooms, and that there was no other way for us than to wait for them to come out, however tiresome it might be. Thus we patiently waited till five in the morning.

Hardly had Red-shirt and Noda, the Clown, come out of the saloon before we stealthily followed them like blood hounds. It was too early for the first train to start. They would have to walk all the way to the castle town. In the outskirts of the town of hot springs, there are rows of cedar trees planted on both sides of the road for about a block with rice fields right and left. Beyond this, you will see peasants' lowly thatched cottages scattered here and there. There runs through the corn fields a dyke leading to the castle town. Once out of the town of hot springs, we might overtake them any place, but if possible it was most desirable to catch them where the rows of cedars stood. In and out of sight of them we followed. No sooner had we got outside the town than we pursued them at a quick pace and came upon them like a tempest. Sudden terror made one of them look to see what the matter was, when the big heavy hand of Porcupine caught him by the shoulder. It was Red-shirt. The frightened Noda was about to run away from the scene, but I stood before him like a wall.

"Are you not dean, and how could you dare stay over night at Kadoya?" pre-emptorily demanded Porcupine of Red-shirt without a moment's delay.

"Is there any rule or regulation, sir, prohibiting a dean from lodging at Kadoya, a hotel?" he answered in as polite a way as ever, but his countenance betrayed fear; it was a little pale.

"You were the man who said it was detrimental to the discipline of the school for teachers to frequent the buckwheat shop or *tempura* stand, and how dared you stay over night at the hotel with a dancing girl?" demanded Porcupine again. Noticing that the Clown was watching for a chance to escape, I interrupted and roared out, "How dared you call me a 'boy rascal?'" "No," he answered, "I did not mean you, not at all. I meant somebody else." Thus the brazen-faced artist tried to excuse himself. Just then I became aware that I was still holding my sleeves with both my hands. This I had to do to enable me to run faster, for the eggs in the sleeves would have been a great hindrance. Naturally my hands went into the sleeves; brought out two of the eggs; the missiles found their way to the face of the flatterer; the eggs broke; the yolk ran down from his nose in big drops. Frightened to death, Noda called out for help and fell on his back, a cry of terror escaping from his lips. True I had bought the eggs to eat and had not carried them all the way in my sleeves in order that I might use them as missiles, but anger made me lance them at the face of the Clown. I did not know they were so effective a weapon until he fell down on his back. Success made me throw the rest of the eggs with the cry, "You brute!" at the poor artist, whose face was all painted with yellow.

While I was thus carrying on an egg fight, Porcupine was cross-examining Red-shirt.

"But have you any proof I have stayed over night at the hotel with a dancing girl?"

"These eyes of mine saw your paramour going into Kadoya in the evening. To fool me is impossible."

"Deception of any sort is uncalled for, my dear Mr. Hotta. We two, Mr. Yoshikawa and I lodged there. That's all. Whether a geisha went into the hotel or not was not our business at all."

"Hold your tongue, you cursed knave!" thundered out Porcupine and gave him a good blow upon the cheek. "Violence! Outrageous!" Red-shirt cried, "It is not lawful to resort to force without appealing to reason."

"Violence is exactly what you need," exclaimed Porcupine and with this went another blow. "A good thrashing is the only way to chastise such a confirmed ruffian as you." And with this, unnumbered blows were delivered. I did the same with Noda, until at last, crouching down at the roots of the cedar tree, they made no more attempts to run away. I dare say they could not get about, or rather they got dizzy.

"Enough? or more blows?" went another and another blow from us both.

"Enough, no more, thank you," answered the humiliated dean in a pitiful tone. I asked the Clown if he was satisfied, too, and he answered, "Yes, fully satisfied."

"Great ruffians you two are, and we have inflicted a Heaven-commissioned punishment upon you both," said Porcupine, "Try to be better men henceforward. Justice will never permit a bad man to go unpunished, however eloquently he may defend himself." Red-shirt and Noda both held their tongues; probably exhaustion was the cause of their silence.

"I shall neither flee nor hide," said Porcupine, "I shall be in Minatoya at the beach till five this evening. Send police or any one you like if you have any business with me." I followed his example and said that I too would never fly or hide, but wait right on with Mr. Hotta in the same place to give them time to go to the police station to make a complaint against me if they had mind to do so. Thus leaving them, we briskly went on our way.

I got home a little before seven in the morning. Hardly had I got into my room before I began to pack up all my things. The old landlady, greatly amazed, asked me what I was going to do. "Well, my dear old lady," I answered, "I am going back to Tokyo to fetch my wife." I paid the bill; lost no time in getting into the train; put up at Minatoya at the beach. Porcupine was found fast asleep upstairs. I wished to write my resignation in proper form, yet not knowing how to do it, I scratched off a letter as follows:

I resign and go back to Tokyo. Circumstances make me do so.

Yours truly,
B.

This was properly addressed to Principal Badger and sent him by mail.

Six P.M. was the scheduled hour at which the steamer was to weigh anchor. Porcupine and I, out of exhaustion, had a dream-less slumber right on till two in the afternoon. On awaking, we asked the maid if the police had called and she answered in the negative. "Neither Red-shirt nor Noda has then made any complaint against us, it seems," we said and had a hearty laugh.

That evening we bade our last adieu to that wretched place. The farther we were from the shore, the better we felt. We took an express from Kobe to Tokyo. When we alighted at Shimbashi, we felt as if we had come out of hell into a world of light. There we parted, Porcupine and I, and I have had no chance to meet him ever since.

To return to Kiyo, the nurse. No sooner had I arrived at To-kyo than, without calling at my boardinghouse, I proceeded to Kiyo's carrying my carpet bags all the way. My ringing voice, "Here I am, my Kiyo," at the entrance called forth from the back room the old woman who welcomed me with, "O my young master, how have I longed to see you!" Tears ran down from her cheeks in big warm drops. Extreme happiness made me tell her that I would never go into the country again, but have my home with her in Tokyo.

Not long after, I got a position as an assistant technician in the Street Car Company through the kind offices of a certain friend. Twenty-five yen was my salary; six of it went for house rent. Kiyo seemed quite satisfied and happy even with the house with no portico, but in the second month of the year, the poor woman succumbed to pneumonia. The day before she breathed her last she called me to her bedside and requested me if she could be permitted for mercy's sake to be buried in our family graveyard, so that she might there contentedly wait for me to come. Therefore, Yōgen-ji, Kobinata, is her last resting place. May she rest in peace!